A Fox Under My Jacket

Paul and Jo are country boys who have come to live in London much against their will. They hate it – until Paul discovers Hampstead Heath and the family of foxes that lives there.

A Fox Under My Jacket is Harriet Graham's first children's novel. She has worked in a kindergarten in India, for a literary agent and for a repertory company. She lives in London with her actor/writer husband, John Graham, and their two sons.

Harriet Graham

A fox under my jacket

Cover illustration by Priscilla Clive
Text illustrations by James Hunt

A Piccolo Book
Pan Books Ltd London and Sydney
in association with William Heinemann Ltd

First published 1971 by William Heinemann Ltd
This edition published 1972 by Pan Books Ltd,
Cavaye Place, London SW10 9PG,
in association with William Heinemann Ltd
2nd printing 1975
© Harriet Graham 1971
ISBN 0 330 23339 4

Printed in Great Britain by
Richard Clay (The Chaucer Press) Ltd, Bungay, Suffolk

CONTENTS

For Charles and Matthew

1

The End of Everything

Paul looked once again at the clock which stood above the classroom door. Still five minutes to go before the bell rang. The hard knot of excitement which had been inside him when he woke that morning, and which had been growing all day, was now so huge that he felt as though he would soon explode if the bell did not ring.

On the other side of the courtyard Paul could see Jo's classroom window, but he couldn't see Jo without standing up because his younger brother's desk was at the far side of the room. Paul looked at the clock again. One minute to four.

'I hope you will all have good holidays,' Miss Humphreys said, glancing at the clock herself and picking up her black leather handbag. 'There's the bell now. No stampeding please.'

Paul knew that there was no point in joining the headlong rush for the classroom door. Jo would be the last one out; he always was. Anyway Paul still had one thing left to do.

He looked round at the empty classroom. The graph which they had made during the maths lessons was still there on the wall, and the photographs of British birds still looked down from beside the blackboard. The date was still there, on the blackboard, in Miss Humphrey's clear, round writing. Thursday, March 24th. But none of it mattered any more, Paul thought.

The holidays had begun at last, and tomorrow he was going back to Martinford.

He lifted the lid of his desk and took out his home-made calendar. There was just one day left to cross off; one empty square in the bottom right-hand corner. Back at half-term Paul had drawn a red line round that square. Now he looked at it thoughtfully and took a red pencil from his box. Slowly he coloured in the square, so that no white showed at all. Then he put the pencil back in the box, and put the box in his satchel. The calendar was complete and he wouldn't be needing it any more. He took it over to the waste-paper basket, tore it into tiny pieces and dropped them in.

Outside in the playground Jo was waiting for him beside the drinking fountain. Jo was two years younger than Paul, and though he was shorter he was wiry and tough. He had an upturned nose and very wide blue eyes, and his mouth, so his mother said, was as large as a letter-box. Altogether Jo had a cheerful, forthright appearance which often made people smile when they looked at him. Paul was not at all like his brother, for he was lean and bony where Jo was square, and his eyes, which were grey, had a reflective look, as though he was all the time thinking of something which was going on a long way away. It was only when Paul smiled that his face lost its serious look and his eyes sparkled with fun. But for the last few months no one had seen Paul smile very much.

'It's not working and I'm thirsty,' Jo said as Paul came up. He was leaning over the drinking fountain pressing the metal button with the palm of his hand.

'You're always thirsty,' said Paul. 'I'm going so you'll have to catch me up,' and he started towards the gate.

It was very quiet now that everyone had gone. Paul had always hated the playground, and as he looked around at it he suddenly knew why. 'No green,' he muttered. 'No trees, no grass, nothing.' At the gate he stopped and cast a final look at the bleak asphalt square, and the high brick walls which surrounded it. Then he went out, leaving Jo to follow.

It usually took the boys about twenty minutes to walk home. Paul, because he hated the walk through the noisy, dusty streets, walked quickly, looking at the paving stones passing beneath his feet. But he had to keep stopping to wait for Jo who liked to dawdle and look at things on the way. There was the house where the grey cat lived, and if it sat sunning itself on the wall, as it often did, Jo would stop and talk to it. Farther up the hill was the little sweet shop where they bought sugar shrimps, two for a penny, or sometimes, when they had enough money, ice creams.

At the top of the hill they had to cross the main road before turning into Brownlow Street. Their house was Number 35. It was red brick, just like all the other houses in the street, and the rooms were small and dark. The best thing about their house was that they had a bigger garden than anyone else in the road. They had a side gate too. That was because Number 35 was at the end. But Paul and Jo had been brought up in the country, where there is always plenty of room for everyone.

When they first moved into 35 Brownlow Street their mother had taken them straight out to the back garden to show it to them. She had pointed out the rambler rose which grew against the wall, and the old apple tree by the wooden fence. 'That will be all pink blossom in the spring,' she said. To Paul the garden just looked like a

9

dank, muddy strip of ground, hardly long enough to play football on. He thought of the woods and fields which they had left behind at Martinford, and standing there on the patchy turf he decided that he hated London and everything about it.

It was then that Jo had found the shed. It was at the end of the garden, and partly hidden by the apple tree. Inside it was dry and empty, except for some shelves running round the walls. It was the kind of shed where one might keep gardening tools and flower pots; or, thought Paul, where one might keep rabbits if one lived in the country.

Jo was excited. 'We could have a camp here,' he said. 'Make a list of rules and pin them up. What do you think, Paul? And we could keep cups and plates on the shelves.' But Paul was silent. One dirty old shed wasn't going to make up for all that they had left behind, and he couldn't think what Jo was getting so excited about.

Jo went to fetch his mother, leaving Paul alone in the shed. 'Can we have it – for our own I mean?' Jo asked, diving past her to stand in the middle of the shed as though to prove his ownership.

'I can't think what they wanted with a shed in a garden this size anyway,' their mother said, peering in and wrinkling her nose in distaste.

'I mean with a key and padlock, so that no one else can come in,' Jo went on, making quite sure that his mother understood.

'Yes, yes, Jo,' she laughed. 'Yes. You can.' Jo gave a whoop and dashed outside, but Paul didn't say anything. After a moment his mother came across and put her arm round him. 'Cheer up, Paul,' she said, giving him a little shake. 'I know it's not the same as Martinford, but we'll soon get used to it. You'll see.'

'I won't,' said Paul fiercely. 'I never will.'

That was more than three months ago, and nothing had happened since then to make Paul change his mind. Even at school things went wrong for him. The other boys laughed at his country accent to begin with, and then, after a while, they simply ignored him. Paul felt isolated and lonely. They treated Jo in the same way, but Jo was more independent and didn't seem to mind. Anyway he had his shed. Paul obstinately refused to take any part in the shed, and after a while Jo gave up asking him. At Martinford they had always done things together, and it wasn't long before Paul knew that he had been wrong. But he was too proud to ask Jo if he could join in after all, so he just moped around, or lay on his bedroom floor reading comics until it was time to go to bed. One day seemed to merge into the next in a grey haze of misery, and after a while Paul's mood affected them all.

'It's hardly worth having a grand new job if I have to come home to long faces every night,' Mr Tomlinson grumbled. 'Isn't that boy ever going to settle down?' Mrs Tomlinson shook her head.

'I don't know,' she said. 'But we can't go on like this. We'll have to think of something.' She missed Martinford too, and she knew how Paul felt. In the end it was she who had suggested that Paul and Jo should go down there for the holidays and stay with their grandmother. At first Mr Tomlinson had objected.

'Won't your mother find them rather a handful? She's not as young as she was.' Mrs Tomlinson's face had crinkled into a smile when she heard that.

'Don't you worry,' she had said. 'Mother will know now to manage. Anyway they'll be out in the fields all

11

day. She'll hardly see them.' In the end Mr Tomlinson had agreed to the idea.

'But after that Paul will really have to settle down,' he said.

When Paul heard the news he was overjoyed. To him, going to Martinford meant going home. At last he had something to look forward to. He made the calendar and ticked off the days, one by one. Slowly they crept past, and slowly the calendar filled up, until, at last, there were no more squares left.

And now, walking home from school, Paul knew that this time tomorrow he would be in Martinford. Outside the sweet shop Jo caught up with him.

'Hey,' he said, 'wait for me. I want to buy some shrimps.'

'All right,' said Paul. 'But hurry up. I want to get home.' Jo disappeared into the darkness of the shop and Paul leant against the railings, looking back down the hill at the endless rows of houses which stretched away as far as he could see. On the road the traffic roared up the hill, changing gear by the bus stop.

Three boys came out of the shop. 'Linda White had a fright, in the middle of the night,' they sang. Paul recognized them, but they ignored him and walked on up the hill, singing ... 'Saw a ghost eating toast, half way up a lamp post.' Paul knew they were members of Michael Skinner's gang. He turned his back on them, pretending he was glad that they hadn't said anything to him, and peered through the railings. What did he care, when tomorrow he would be in Martinford. There was a narrow gap between the sweet shop and the next house. As the sound of the chanting died away he was suddenly aware that beyond the gap there were trees. Trees, and, unbelievably, what looked like fields. He blinked. Perhaps the green was a mirage. But when he opened his eyes again it was still there. A great rolling field.

'Hey, Jo! Look at this,' he said, pointing in the direction of the field.

Jo was counting out the shrimps. 'What?'

'That,' Paul said. 'Over there . . .'

'Oh *that*,' said Jo, looking up. 'That's Hampstead Heath.'

'I never noticed it before,' Paul said. 'What is it anyway?'

Jo shrugged and put a sugar shrimp in his mouth. 'Just a park I suppose. Only bigger. We pass the notice every day.'

'What notice?'

'Look, what does it matter? We're going to Granny's tomorrow anyway. Here, do you want these or not?' Paul took the shrimps which Jo held out for him, counted them and put them in his pocket. Jo was right, he thought, what did it matter? However big it was, it was still only a park and tomorrow they would be in the country. But there was always next term.

'Not just a lot of swings and sand pits is it?' he asked Jo anxiously.

'I don't think so,' said Jo. 'The others go there often.'

'What others?'

'Oh you know,' said Jo impatiently. 'Others at school.'

Paul glanced at Jo and saw that he had that shut in look which meant that he wasn't going to answer any more questions for the moment. So he put a shrimp in his mouth, chewed it slowly, and thought.

There had been a great field of grass. He had seen it. Jo said it was a big park, but how big? Two miles, or

13

six miles, or even more? Perhaps there would be trees to climb, and hedges and ... He frowned. No. It couldn't possibly be like that. That was the country, and they were in the middle of London.

But tomorrow they would be in the country. Three weeks of freedom lay ahead, and Hampstead Heath could wait.

'Race you home,' he said to Jo as they turned the corner into Brownlow Street.

Jo was just ahead as the two boys burst through the side gate and ran towards the back door of Number 35.

'Yahoo!' called Jo. 'Mum. We're back.'

Their mother was sitting by the table which was laid for tea, and Paul knew at once that something was wrong. She didn't smile as she usually did when they came in, and she spoke quite sharply.

'You can stop all that noise, Jo. And go and wash your hands, they're filthy, and sticky too.' Jo opened his mouth to protest, and then changed his mind and went upstairs.

Paul went on standing, looking at his mother. He wanted to ask what had happened, but he didn't have the courage. The room suddenly seemed very quiet. Without looking at him, his mother picked up the teapot and began to pour out the tea.

'Can I take my football tomorrow?' Paul asked at last, unable to bear the silence any longer. 'I don't suppose it will go in my case, but I could carry it.' Mrs Tomlinson frowned, and then she put the teapot down and sighed.

'Look, Paul,' she said, gently, 'you're not going to Martinford after all. You can't. They've just phoned me from the Cottage Hospital. Granny's fallen down and broken her leg.'

14

2

The Beginning of Everything

More than anything else, after hearing the news, Paul wanted to be alone, so that night he went to bed early, long before Jo. He fell at once into a troubled sleep, through which he heard his parents' voices, and the occasional clatter of dishes in the kitchen below. The voices became mixed up with his dreams after a while, and later, when he woke, the murmuring had stopped, but the wind, which had risen, rattled the windows and blew in eerie gusts down the chimney. He slept again.

Paul dreamt that he had arrived at Martinford, but all around his grandmother's cottage there were red-brick houses, and although he searched and searched he could find no fields, and no trees. The lane leading up to the hill had gone, and where it should have been there was a high brick wall.

When Paul opened his eyes he found that his face was wet with tears. He brushed them angrily away and rolled over on his back.

Through the gap in the curtains he could see a patch of cold, blue sky, but he knew it must still be very early. Jo usually woke first, but he was still asleep, deep under the bedclothes with only a spike of hair showing. Outside it was very quiet. Far away Paul heard the rumble of an early bus. The only other sound was made by the pigeons on the roof of the house, chuckling among themselves.

He rolled over and closed his eyes again. If he could go back to sleep he wouldn't have to think about not going to Martinford. Not yet, anyway.

But he couldn't go back to sleep. The sun had come out now, and was shining through the gap in the curtains. 'If I was at Martinford,' Paul thought angrily, 'I'd get up and go for a walk. But there's no point in London. Just streets.'

Then, quite suddenly, he remembered the great, green rolling field and he sat up with a jerk. He hadn't thought about it since yesterday, but that was something, that field, and all those trees. Hampstead Heath. If it was really big, well, it wouldn't be the same as the country, he knew that, but it would be better than nothing. It would be somewhere to go that wasn't just streets.

He sat up and looked across at Jo, wondering whether to wake him up and talk to him about it. But Jo hadn't seemed particularly interested yesterday, and Paul knew that he'd never been there.

All at once Paul knew what he would do. He would go now, by himself, while everyone else was still asleep, and he would have a look at Hampstead Heath and see just how big it was. Then he would come back and tell Jo about it. He grinned to himself, and climbing out of bed he began to dress.

Through the window he could see the pigeons pecking about on the grass, and he heard a milk float rattle by on the road. He would have to hurry, he thought.

He went very slowly and quietly down the stairs so as not to wake anyone, and once safely in the kitchen he looked at the clock. It was half past six; still another quarter of an hour before his parents' alarm clock would go off. The table was all ready, laid for breakfast, and Paul drank some milk from the jug, wiping his mouth

16

with his sleeve. Then, as an afterthought, he took a piece of bread and spread it thickly with butter and jam, leaving the knife in the jam pot.

Holding the bread and jam between his teeth Paul undid the bolts on the back door and slipped out into the garden.

'Wish we had a dog,' he thought. A dog would have been company on a morning like this. Dogs didn't ask questions, and they were always glad to go out on an expedition. His grandmother had a dog called Skipper. But Skipper was getting old now. Paul would have liked a mongrel with big brown eyes, and a tail like a plume, who would run beside him when he went out, and bark and jump, and fetch sticks from the water. He might have had such a dog if they had stayed at Martinford. But not in London.

Outside the air smelt clean and fresh, but it was very cold. Brownlow Street was deserted, except for the milk float at the end of the road. It must be the same one that he had heard when he was dressing, Paul thought. He pushed the last of the bread and jam into his mouth as he drew level with the float.

'Up early aren't you?' said the milkman pleasantly. Paul nodded.

'I like it,' he said, still chewing. 'It's quiet.'

'Quite right,' agreed the milkman. 'Best part of the day. Bit nippy this morning, though.' He took three pints of milk from the crate and went whistling up the path of Number 8; Paul inspected the inside of the float.

'Holidays started have they?' asked the milkman when he came back. Paul nodded. 'Well, if you're up as early as this every day, you'll be able to help with the round, won't you?'

17

'Could I?' Paul was pleased with the idea.

'Joking I was,' he smiled, taking a carton of cream from the refrigerator at the side of the float. 'We're not allowed to have kids on the round, see. Pity I think. A bit of hard work and you wouldn't all be hanging round so much.'

'Oh, I'm not hanging round,' said Paul quickly, beginning to move off. 'I'm going to Hampstead Heath.'

'Oh yes,' the milkman nodded.

'Do you know it?' Paul asked. The milkman leant against the float, still holding the cream.

'Hang on a moment,' he said slowly. 'You must be from Number 35.'

'That's right,' said Paul.

'Moved in about three months ago. You're new to London aren't you?'

'Yes,' said Paul. 'We used to live in the country.'

'Ever been to the Heath before?' asked the milkman. Paul shook his head. 'Know the way?'

'I think so,' said Paul doubtfully.

'Tell you what,' said the milkman, 'you hang on here while I do the last two houses, and then I'll give you a lift. The shop's right by the Heath and I'm going back there anyway.'

'Thanks very much,' said Paul, turning quite pink with pleasure. He had never ridden in a milk float before, and he climbed in quickly and perched himself on the brown leather seat before the milkman could change his mind.

'What brought you to London?' the milkman asked, coming back and climbing in beside Paul.

'My dad was offered a better job in the London office,' Paul explained. 'More money.' The float made a low whining noise as they set off, and the crates rattled gently in the back as they swayed round the corner into the main road.

Half way down the hill, just after they had passed the sweet shop, the milkman put out his hand and signalled that he was going to turn right.

'The dairy's just down here,' he said, as they rattled along the small street. 'And there, at the end, is the Heath.'

Paul looked ahead where the milkman was pointing. He could see three metal posts, and above and beyond them, trees.

'Here we are,' said the milkman, putting on the brake.

'Thanks for the lift,' said Paul, climbing out. 'It was great.'

'That's all right,' said the milkman. 'Don't get lost.' And he began to unload the crates.

Paul walked slowly up the street towards the iron posts. Above the rattle of the milk bottles he heard a blackbird singing. The little road had small white houses on either side of it, and in the front gardens the daffodils and crocuses were coming out. Paul began to run.

Beyond the iron posts the houses ended, and there, stretching out before him, as far as he could see, was grass, with trees, and little paths, and birds hopping about all over the place, and farther away a great rise of green hill crowned with more trees. He stopped, and looked at it all. Never for a moment had he thought that the Heath could be this big. There wasn't a single person in sight. Just him, and all this rolling green. He looked back once at the little street, and then with a great whoop of joy, he ran onto the Heath.

The wind swept over the Heath and whistled past him as he pelted down the path. It blew his hair about, and nipped his ears and nose, but it smelt clean and fresh. It smelt like country air. Around him the birds flew into the bushes with startled cries as he sped past, and the sun glistened on the grass which swayed and rippled under the wind's touch. Paul soon left the main path and splashed across small, muddy puddles left by the night's rain as he made his way towards the high, green hill crowned with trees.

The hill was steep, much steeper than it looked, and long before he reached the top he had to slow down because of the stitch in his side. But nothing could stifle the feeling of happiness inside him. When at last, breathless, Paul reached the summit, he gasped as he looked about him.

'There's miles of it,' he murmured, 'miles and miles of it.'

Looking back the way he had come he could see the path leading all the way to the iron posts where the houses began; and he could see other houses too, and streets curving round the bottom of the Heath like arms. But to right and left, and in front of him there was hardly a house to be seen. Far away in the distance another hill was dotted with houses set among trees, and two or three tall church spires rose above the branches; but between him and the hill the ground fell away into great expanses of grass, dotted with small clumps of bushes, and here and there a line of trees. Down there, too, was a pond, beside which a man and his dog were walking: the only other human in sight.

Suddenly there was space again. Room to ride a bicycle. Room to play football. Room to run and shout and not bump into other people. He could see the sky again, and the racing clouds were no longer hidden by chimney stacks. There was silence too. Apart from the

20

sound of the wind no noise disturbed this place. And down there in the hollows they could make camps, and climb trees and have picnics.

From up here London looked different. It was no longer grim and ugly as he had always thought it. It was beautiful. And all the time they had been in London it

had just been sitting here, all this open space and quiet and green, just waiting for them to find it. If only they had known.

Then Paul smiled to think of himself up there on the hill, and Jo still at home in bed. He had been the one to find it. He, Paul Tomlinson.

'Just wait till I get home and tell Jo,' he said aloud, for there was no one to hear him talking to himself. 'Just wait till I tell him,' he shouted.

3

A Fresh Start

At a quarter to seven, sharp, the alarm clock rang at 35 Brownlow Street. Mrs Tomlinson, who was already half awake, nudged her husband to tell him that it was time to get up, and then climbed out of bed. Mr Tomlinson watched her out of one eye as she put on her old, blue dressing-gown, and then, pulling the sheet over his head, he went back to sleep.

In the next room Jo had woken up too. The first thing he noticed when he opened his eyes was Paul's empty bed, and he sat up at once and began to feel about under his pillow, which was where he kept the key of the shed. Jo had become very possessive about his shed lately, and his first thought was that Paul had sneaked off to have a look at it without telling him. The key had slipped down inside his pillow case during the night, and when Jo at last found it, he heaved a great sigh of relief.

If Paul wasn't in the shed, he was probably in the garden, Jo thought. Through the window he could see a sleek black cat on the fence watching the pigeons on the grass, but there was no sign of Paul.

In the country they used to leave notes for one another, like 'Gone to the big field', or 'Gone to the wood'. But Paul hadn't left a note.

Jo was puzzled. It was so unlike Paul to go off without saying a word, and he began to wonder whether

Granny's broken leg, and not going to Martinford could have anything to do with Paul's disappearance. He had certainly been in a funny mood last night, Jo thought; he had gone to bed so early, long before he was told to.

Gradually the idea came to Jo that Paul had run away. During the first weeks in London they had talked about it. There was an old house in the woods above Martinford where, Paul had said, you could live for weeks without being discovered. But surely, Jo thought, he would never have gone without saying a word about it. Jo climbed miserably back into bed and lay thinking.

The Tomlinsons had tea in bed every morning, rain or shine, because Mrs Tomlinson said that it helped them to get up in a good mood, and that was worth a great deal.

'Someone's been downstairs helping themselves to bread and jam,' she said as she came in. Jo saw her look across at the empty bed. 'And where's Paul?' she asked.

'I don't know,' said Jo. 'When I woke up he'd gone.'

'Gone? But it's only seven o'clock. Where can he have gone at this time of the morning?'

'I don't know.'

'He'll be down in that shed, I expect,' said Mrs Tomlinson handing Jo his tea.

'No, he's not,' Jo shook his head. 'Because I've got the key here, and you can't get in without that.'

'Well, then I daresay he's gone for a walk. Anyway, you drink that up and don't spill it on the sheets,' and Mrs Tomlinson left the room quickly so that Jo wouldn't see that she was worried.

When Paul came back, if he came back at all, Jo thought gloomily as he began to dress, then he would

23

be specially kind to him. For a start he would show him the shed. That would cheer him up.

While Jo was upstairs dressing, Mrs Tomlinson was in the kitchen frying bacon and thinking about Paul. He still hadn't come back and because she was worried about him she kept going to the window to see if he was coming through the garden, and that meant she only had half an eye on the bacon. Then she discovered that she had forgotten to put any plates in to warm, and by the time she had fetched them, and lit the oven, the bacon had begun to burn in the frying pan. That was the final straw, and Mrs Tomlinson let out a shriek just as her husband came into the kitchen.

'Hey, what's up?' asked Mr Tomlinson. 'Did you get out of bed the wrong side this morning?' He was a large, comfortable man, and he said it quite jokingly, but Mrs Tomlinson was in no mood for jokes that morning.

'Better than not getting up at all,' she snapped. 'Do you think I've got nothing better to do than cook breakfast for people who aren't here to eat it? And *you're* late too,' she said to Jo, who was trying to slip into his place without being seen. 'I just hope you remembered to wash your face before you came down.' And she banged their plates down in front of them and then began to pour out the tea, making a good deal of clatter and looking more flustered than ever. If Paul didn't come back soon Mrs Tomlinson knew that she'd have to speak to her husband about it, and then he'd be late for work.

Just then, Paul, quite unaware of all the trouble he was causing that morning, burst through the side gate and raced across the garden. He was red in the face with all the excitement and fresh air, and his eyes were sparkling. Jo could see at once that something good had happened to him; and Mrs Tomlinson who had been about to fire off a string of angry questions stood, holding the teapot in one hand, and stared at him. She could hardly believe her eyes. Paul actually looked happy. She hadn't seen him look like that for months, not since they moved to London, and in a moment all her anxiety and irritation vanished.

'Sorry I'm late,' said Paul. 'I went for a walk.'

'Where to?' Jo asked.

'Just a walk,' Paul said, picking up his knife and fork.

'Well, wherever he went it seems to have given him an appetite,' Mrs Tomlinson said as she watched him tucking into his bacon and fried bread. 'So you just get on with your own breakfast Jo, and don't ask questions.'

Paul could feel his brother staring at him across the table, but he wasn't going to be hurried. Jo would have to wait until he had finished his breakfast. It was only when he was sure that he had had enough to eat that Paul sat back in his chair and said, rather loudly, 'I found something when I was out this morning.'

Jo stopped chewing and looked at him, and his mother sat forward in her chair and said expectantly, 'Yes?' Even his father looked up from his paper.

'Not so much a thing,' said Paul, seeing that they were all looking at him. 'More a place.'

'Whatever is the boy on about?' Mr Tomlinson asked, rattling his paper. 'Thing ... place ...' Mrs Tomlinson waved her hand at him to tell him not to interrupt and said, 'Well, go on ...'

'Yes. GO ON, Paul!' said Jo.

Paul took a deep breath. 'It's a sort of park I suppose. Only it isn't. I mean – it's like a park, only bigger. Enormous. Like the country,' he finished rather lamely.

Jo was very disappointed. Paul hadn't run away after all, and he hadn't even found anything interesting, like a chimpanzee, or a five pound note. He'd only been to Hampstead Heath.

'Is that all?' he asked scornfully.

'Well, you've never been there,' Paul flashed.

'Quiet, boys,' Mrs Tomlinson said. 'I've never seen any park like that,' she went on, turning back to Paul.

'You can't see it,' Paul explained, 'because of all the houses. But when you get there you can't think how you missed it, because it's so enormous. And it's not like a proper park at all. It's wild, with trees and hills. You could ride a bicycle there.'

Mr and Mrs Tomlinson glanced at one another across the table, and Mr Tomlinson said, 'Now Paul, is this one of your tall stories? Your mother and I have said we're very sorry about the bikes, but it isn't safe in London.'

'It would be there.'

'Is it really that big?' Jo asked.

'Huge. You wait till you see it.'

'Well, I still can't think how we've never noticed it if it's that big,' said Mrs Tomlinson doubtfully.

Mr Tomlinson stood up. 'You'd better get Paul to explain,' he said. 'If it's as big as he thinks,' he winked at his wife, 'then it's sure to be marked on that map I gave you. I must go now or I'll be late.'

Mrs Tomlinson followed her husband into the hall, and helped him on with his coat. 'Well, there's one thing,' she said, 'Paul hasn't mentioned Martinford this morning, and that's a good sign.'

'I always said he'd settle down all right,' said Mr Tomlinson cheerfully.

In the kitchen Paul looked at Jo across the table. 'I

don't suppose you believe me either,' he said.

'Yes I do,' said Jo stoutly, suddenly remembering his resolve to be specially kind to Paul.

'Will you come then?'

Jo nodded. 'Of course. And I want you to see my shed too.'

'I'd like to, if you want me to. Sorry if I've been ... you know ...' Now that he had found the Heath everything suddenly seemed different and he wanted to say sorry to Jo for a lot of things, but he didn't quite know how to do it.

'That's all right,' said Jo quickly. 'Shall we go?'

'Before you two disappear,' said their mother, coming back into the kitchen with the bus map, 'I want to know where this place is.' She pushed all the cups and plates down to one end of the table and spread out the map. 'Where are we?'

'Here,' said Paul, leaning over the map and putting his finger on the black cross which his father had made to show roughly where their house was. Jo leant over the map as well. The scale was quite small, because the map showed the bus routes for the whole of London. 'Look,' said Paul. 'There's the hill we walk up and down to school, and there –' he jabbed his finger on a small patch of green, 'see, it says, "Hampstead Heath".'

'It doesn't look all that big to me.' His mother screwed her head round to read the print. 'It's not that park up the hill is it?' There was a small park not far from them. It was surrounded by a wire fence and had grass you couldn't walk on. They sometimes went there on Sunday afternoons, and Paul hated it.

Of course Mrs Tomlinson wasn't used to reading maps. If Mr Tomlinson had been there he would have seen at once that the scale on the bus map was very

27

small, and would have guessed that Hampstead Heath was several miles across and quite big enough to get lost in if you didn't know your way about. He would have seen, too, that if you were to walk from one side of the Heath to the other, then you would arrive in quite a different part of London. But Mr Tomlinson wasn't there, and all that his wife saw was a rather small patch of green on a large map, and in her mind's eye she conjured up a space about the size of a village green, with a duck pond in the middle. Paul was pleased, she thought, glancing at him, and that was the main thing. He needed something to make up for not going to Martinford, and now that the holidays were here, and the weather milder they both needed somewhere to play. This park he had found looked as though it had turned up at just the right moment.

'I still can't think how I've never noticed it before.'

'Well, you never go that way,' said Paul. 'When you go to the shops it's the opposite direction.'

'I knew it was there,' said Jo. 'But I've been busy with the shed.'

'That shed!' said his mother, folding up the map. 'Well, if you are going out to play, mind the roads.'

4

The Kite

Before they set off for the Heath Jo led Paul down the garden path towards the shed. He didn't say a word when they reached the door, but delved in his pocket for the key, and looked round before fitting it into the lock, just to make sure no one was watching. Mrs Tomlinson was washing up, and all the other gardens were deserted. Only the black cat eyed them steadily from her post on the wall. Jo pushed open the door and stood aside to let Paul go in first.

The last time Paul had been inside the shed it had seemed very dark and gloomy, and covered with cobwebs. But in the three months since they had moved to London Jo had worked hard. He had found that some of the old paint tins in the corner still had something in them; there was a brush too, a bit stiff, but he managed to use it. By mixing together what was left in all the tins Jo made a light grey; there was just enough to cover the walls with one coat and it had made the shed much brighter. The small tin of red paint which he had found tucked away at the back of the pile of other paint pots, he used for the shelves.

'It's great, Jo,' said Paul, looking round in admiration. 'I like the table too.' Jo had made the table from a couple of orange boxes with a long strip of wood nailed across the top. Two smaller boxes served for stools.

'And the carpet,' Jo said, just in case Paul hadn't

noticed. 'D'you like the carpet?' It was an old strip with holes in it which someone down the road had thrown out, but Jo was proud of the air of luxury which it gave to the shed. On the wall by the window was Jo's list of rules. It began:

1. The door must always be kept locked.

The 'always' was underlined several times.

'And over here,' said Jo, 'this is my corner for my special things.' He paused, looking at Paul. 'You could have the other end if you liked.'

'Great.' Paul nodded enthusiastically. 'We could put up a dividing bit in the middle.'

'Good idea,' said Jo with a grin, pleased by Paul's interest. 'Of course,' he went on, 'I haven't got many things down here. Just a few note-books and some string – things like that.'

'What's that?' Paul asked, pointing to a large object wrapped in paper.

'That's my kite,' said Jo. He took it off the shelf and unwrapped it proudly.

Jo had been saving up for the kite since half-term and he had only just collected enough money to buy the one he wanted. The red and green linen had a crisp new smell about it, and the small pieces of material which ran down the tail were still snow white. It was the first kite which Jo had ever bought, and he had intended to fly it at Martinford. The hill above their grandmother's cottage was a perfect place for kite flying.

'Rotten about Granny, isn't it,' said Jo sadly. 'I don't suppose I'll ever be able to fly it now.'

'There's always the summer holidays.' said Paul. 'A broken leg's not much, is it – she'll be better by then.'

'It's a long time to wait,' said Jo. 'How would you

like to wait all that time?' Paul nodded, knowing how Jo felt. Then his face brightened.

'Wait a moment though. You might not have to wait till the summer. You might be able to fly it today.'

'Today! What a hope!' Jo was scornful.

'You can,' said Paul. 'I'm sure you can. On the Heath. There's a huge hill, and it's windy today too.'

'Are you sure?' Jo asked doubtfully, but he had lost his miserable look. 'Is it a real hill?' Paul nodded.

'I climbed it this morning. The Heath's big enough for anything, you wait till you see it.'

'Hang on a sec,' said Jo. 'We'll want some string.' He rummaged through the pile of odds and ends in the corner and brought out a ball of twine. 'We'd better tie it on here,' he said. 'It'll be easier.' He handed the kite and the string to Paul. 'You do it,' he said. 'You're better at knots than I am.' Paul smiled at him. At Martinford there had been more knots to tie than there were in London, and Paul had always been the one to tie them. Jo grinned back, and for the first time in ages everything seemed to be just right.

It was good, too, Paul thought, to walk down the hill with Jo just as though they were going to school, and to know that they were going instead out onto the Heath. On the way he told Jo about his ride on the milk float, and when they turned into the little street leading to the Heath he stopped for a moment to point out the dairy.

'Where's the Heath then?' Jo asked impatiently.

'There,' said Paul, pointing, and he began to run.

Jo was right behind him as he went past the iron posts and plunged down the path onto the Heath. It all looked just the same as it had done earlier that morning. Trees, grass, bushes, stretching away, but ... Paul stopped.

31

'What's the matter?' Jo asked.

'Well, look,' said Paul crossly. 'All these people. There wasn't anyone this morning.' A woman was wheeling a pram down the path in front of them, and at the bottom of the hill two men were walking along with a dog. Farther away the path was dotted with other figures, and a group of boys were running up the hill kicking a football. All the same Jo thought that Paul was being unreasonable.

'You couldn't expect to have all this to yourself. Not in London. Anyway,' he went on, impatient to reach the top of the hill and try his kite, 'I think it's great.'

'Do you? Do you really?' Paul asked. Jo nodded and Paul, consoled by the remembrance that it was he who had discovered it all, pointed towards the hill.

'When we get to the top you can see how far it stretches,' he said.

'Do you think we'd be allowed to climb the trees?' Jo asked, as they made their way up the hill.

'Don't see why not,' Paul answered. 'And look, there are blackberry bushes over there. It's not a bit like a park, is it?'

As they climbed a train hooted below them, and down on the right they saw a goods train shuffling along the railway line on the perimeter of the Heath. Beyond this the houses began again, stretching away interminably towards the horizon. But to the left there was nothing but grass and trees and open space as far as the eye could see.

'You know,' said Jo thoughtfully when they stood on the summit of the hill, 'I think we could ride bikes here. There are no cars, and it's quite safe.'

It was windy, and although the sun was shining it felt cold. Paul and Jo had almost forgotten what a clean,

32

strong wind felt like, but the kite, which Jo had laid on the ground was making little, fluttering jumps and slides along the grass as though it had a mind of its own and longed to be up in the sky among the racing clouds.

Jo stooped down and picked it up from the grass. He stood for a moment, frowning with concentration and waiting for a good, strong gust of wind. Then he began to run down the slope, tossing the kite up into the air as he ran. It gave a twist, and then fluttered back to the ground. Jo wound up the string and tried again. After several attempts he came slowly back up the slope towards Paul.

'It won't work,' he called.

'Try running the other way,' Paul suggested. 'Perhaps the wind's coming from over there.' Jo put his finger in his mouth and held it up to see which way the wind was blowing. Then he nodded.

'I'll hold the string this time,' Paul said, 'and pay it out as you run.'

This time it worked. The kite snatched itself from Jo's hands, and, caught on an upward gust of wind, rose into the sky. As it went, Paul felt the tug on the string and he began to let out more twine.

'It's up,' Jo yelled, wild with excitement. Paul, too, was thrilled. The kite tugged gently at the string as it rose higher and higher into the air, and he could hardly bear to pass it over to Jo.

'Don't let go,' he warned. 'Keep giving it a little jerk.'

'I know,' said Jo. Anxiously they watched, squinting upwards at the bright sky. 'See, it's all right,' said Jo as the kite rose higher and higher, climbing giddily above the trees and houses. 'It's going like a bird.'

Suddenly, as unpredictably as it had risen, the kite

began to fall back. Jo tugged at the string, jerking it as he had done before, but obstinately the kite swooped and dived, and finally fluttered down to earth, landing in a clump of bushes half way down the hill.

'Doesn't matter,' Jo said. 'Let's go and fetch it.' They made their way down the hill, winding up the string as they went.

'You need a bit of stick to wind the string on to,' Paul said. 'It would be quicker.'

As they approached the clump of bushes they heard voices and a rustling among the branches.

'What's that?' Jo asked.

Paul shrugged. 'Others, I suppose.' They both stopped for a moment to listen, and Paul could make out several forms among the low undergrowth. The kite was sitting on the top of a large hawthorn bush.

'Lucky it didn't go into one of those,' said Jo, pointing at a ring of taller trees farther down the hill.

'We'd never have got it then,' said Paul, reaching out
his hand to take the kite. The noises in the bushes had
stopped, and there was a moment's silence while Paul
tried to grab the kite. Then a head rose up among the
branches just in front of him, and Paul found himself
looking into the dark sullen face of a boy whom he
instantly recognized. It was Michael Skinner.

For a moment the two boys eyed one another silently,
and Paul knew there was going to be trouble. Michael
Skinner must have his whole gang in the bushes with
him, which meant that he and Jo were hopelessly out-
numbered. Worse still, the kite was within Michael
Skinner's grasp.

'You can't come any farther,' said Michael.

'We don't want to come any farther,' Paul answered
steadily. 'Just give us back our kite and we'll go away.'
Michael smiled, and flicked back the lock of dark hair
which fell over his forehead.

'They only want their kite back, and then they'll go away,' he mimicked, and from the bushes there came a chorus of laughter and whistles. Paul flushed, and moved forward.

'No farther,' said Michael.

'Well, give me the kite then,' Paul said, glancing round at Jo.

'Sorry,' said Michael. 'It fell on our hide-out, and that means it's ours. Doesn't it, gang?' There were howls of support from the bushes, and Michael smiled.

'But that's stealing,' Paul said hotly.

'Don't argue,' Jo muttered. 'Just take it.'

'Stealing?' said Michael with mock innocence. 'Findings keepings, isn't it gang?'

'It's mine, you know it is,' Jo shouted, suddenly charging forward, 'and I'm going to get it.'

Then everything began to happen at once. There was a cold click from the bushes, and Jo, looking up, saw that Michael Skinner was holding an open clasp-knife in his hand.

'I wouldn't come any closer,' he said steadily. Paul reached out an arm and grabbed Jo, and as he did so, Michael cut the string, lifted the kite clear from the bushes and disappeared below the branches, taking the kite with him. 'You can keep the string,' he called.

The bushes echoed to the stamp of feet, as the gang ran off, jeering and catcalling as they went. Jo, scarlet with fury, shook himself free from Paul's grasp and charged off in pursuit.

Paul was close behind him as they raced down the hill, and for a few moments all that mattered was the chase, and trying not to trip among the tussocks of grass and the sudden dips and potholes. But all the time the gang were drawing away from Paul and Jo. There were eight of them, Paul could see now, the same old gang from the school playground.

'We'll never catch them,' he panted. But Jo shook his head and ran on.

The ground flattened out now, and across the grass the lines of houses began. The gang raced towards a street, and in a moment they had disappeared round the corner.

When Paul and Jo reached the street, they saw that it curved slowly up and round from the bottom of the Heath, running almost parallel with the railway line. The curve of the street must be hiding the gang from view, because there was no sign of them.

'It's no good, Jo,' Paul gasped, grabbing him. 'What will you do if you catch them?'

'I want my kite back,' Jo yelled, shaking himself free.

'And the knife. What about the knife?' Paul asked. He was frightened, wondering what would happen if they did catch up with the gang. But Jo wouldn't answer. He ran on, scarlet with fury and Paul followed him.

But when they reached the top of the hill Jo stopped and looked about him in bewilderment. The gang had disappeared. There was no sign of them. They had simply vanished.

'They're hiding,' Jo muttered. 'They must be. Listen . . .' and he put a finger to his lips.

Down on the railway line to their left they could hear a train, and in the distance the noise of a pneumatic drill. Farther on, up the street, a telephone rang; but there was no sound of voices, no sound which might have been the gang.

'It's no good,' said Paul after a while. 'I kept trying to tell you.'

37

'They can't have gone far,' Jo answered, his mouth set in an obstinate line. 'I'm going on.'

Where the row of terraced houses ended there was a gap before the next building, which was a tall block of flats, and through the gap the boys looked down to the railway line far below. Between the railway line and the road was a hill covered with bushes and grass.

'There,' Jo pointed. 'I bet they've gone down there.'

'But that's the railway line . . .'

'I bet they have,' Jo persisted. 'And then nipped out again through someone's garden. I'm going down to see if I can find them.'

'You can't, Jo,' said Paul. 'It's probably trespassing.' He looked round, hoping to see a notice that would convince Jo and prevent him from going over the wall. But there was no sign of one.

'Well,' said Jo. 'It doesn't say so, does it? You coming or not?'

Paul followed Jo over the wall and down the hill, expecting at any moment to hear someone shouting at them to stop. But it was very quiet and there was no one about. There was no sign of the gang either. With a look of dogged determination Jo scoured the bushes and undergrowth, but there was no clue, no hint of where the gang might have gone, and there didn't seem to be any way out except the way they had come. At last Jo stood still, his head down, defeated and silent. Then he put his hands over his face and slumped down on the grass.

'The rotten mean cheats,' he muttered between sobs. 'Cheats . . . Cheats . . . Cheats . . .'

5

The Discovery

Paul stood, feeling helpless and miserable, and looked at Jo's hunched up figure on the grass in front of him. When at last Jo stopped crying Paul sat down beside him. Jo hadn't moved; he was still sitting with his knees drawn up, his arms folded across them and his face hidden in his arms.

'Cheer up, Jo,' Paul began cautiously. 'We'll get it back.' There was no answer. He put his hand on Jo's shoulder.

'I hate them,' said Jo, looking up at Paul at last, his face streaked with tears and dirt, his blue eyes blazing. 'It was my kite. Why should they have it? We didn't do anything to them.'

'We'll get it back,' said Paul again, but doubtfully.

'You know we won't,' Jo shouted.

'We might,' said Paul. 'But we'll have to be clever.'

Jo shook his head. 'It's no good. I expect they've already broken it. It's probably lying in a gutter somewhere – or down there on the railway line.'

'They wouldn't *break* it,' said Paul. 'That would be barmy.'

'They will, you know. They're like that in London.'

Paul sighed. Jo was right. He couldn't imagine this happening at Martinford, but in London things were different; even other boys were not the same. He rolled over on his stomach and looked at the grass and twigs.

Only half an hour ago, up there on the hill, it had been all right. The kite had flown like a bird, and with all that open space around them London had seemed like a place where one could be happy after all. Now everything was ruined again.

But the kite was only part of it. Michael Skinner and his gang had won, and Paul knew that he and Jo had been easy meat. Too easy. Paul sensed that from now on it would be open warfare and somehow he and Jo were going to have to fight back or next term Michael Skinner and his gang would be waiting for them round every corner. Paul groaned. He wasn't much of a fighter and he felt himself go cold inside as he remembered the look on Michael Skinner's face as he cut the string on the kite. Why did everything always have to go wrong in London?

'I hate London,' he said. Saying it out loud made him feel better. There was no answer from Jo, but from a clump of bushes nearby a pair of blackbirds began to sing and whistle. The sun was warming Paul's back and the wind seemed to have dropped. It was quiet, too, except for the occasional rattle of a train below them. He lay so still for a few minutes that a thrush hopped quite close to him, its head on one side, and then took fright and scuttered into the nearest bush.

'Tell you what, Jo, I've got about twenty-four pence in my money box,' Paul began. 'You can have that towards a new kite. How much was the kite? Jo?' There was no answer, and Paul sat up and looked round.

Jo had gone. The place where he had been sitting was empty. 'Jo,' he called, standing up. 'Hi! Jo, where are you?' He had been there a moment ago. 'Jo!' he called again. 'Jo!' Paul began to move farther down the bank towards the railway line. His brother couldn't have gone far.

Then, from behind a clump of bushes to his left, he heard Jo's voice. 'It's OK,' he said. 'I'm here.' Paul followed the voice and in a moment he glimpsed Jo's red checked shirt behind the bushes. 'I heard what you said about the money,' said Jo, looking round.

'Why didn't you answer before?' Paul asked crossly.

'I was looking at something,' Jo replied calmly.

'I thought you'd gone,' said Paul. 'You might have answered.'

'Come and look at this,' said Jo.

The bushes behind which they were crouching were about half way between the end of the rows of gardens belonging to the houses above them and the railway line at the bottom of the hill. All but the top storeys of the houses were screened from view by the rise of the hill and by taller trees which grew at the end of the gardens. The undergrowth around the bushes was thick, the grass growing tall and rank after the winter rains, and the branches of the bushes which swept down to the ground around them were just coming into leaf.

Jo pointed to a small dip beneath the bushes. The ground was still covered with a scattering of last year's dead leaves, but, as he looked carefully Paul was aware that there was a flattening of the leaves leading to the dip, as though the ground had been trodden many times.

'And look here,' said Jo, getting on to his stomach and wriggling under the lower branches towards the dip. 'Footprints.'

There was an odd smell under the bushes, too; a smell of dead leaves and damp earth, but of something else as well. At the far side of the dip below the roots of one bush, although it was hard to distinguish because of the dead leaves, was what looked like the entrance to a burrow. In the gloom beneath the branches the two boys looked at one another.

'Dog's been digging,' Paul suggested, but Jo shook his head. 'Well, dogs do dig. They bury bones and things.' Jo didn't answer, but edged himself out backwards and skirted the edge of the bushes. Paul followed.

'Here,' Jo said excitedly. 'Look! Here's another.'

This time it was easier to see, and the two boys sat on their haunches silently, looking at what was unmistakably a burrow.

'It must lead to the other,' Jo muttered. 'And it's used more often too. Look.' In the damp earth at the entrance to the hole there were footprints.

'I told you,' Paul said. 'It's a dog. Look at that print.'

But Jo shook his head, and set off again around the perimeter of the bushes, his head down and his air of concentration giving him the blank look which Paul knew all too well.

In the country Jo had known where every nest in their garden was, what sort of bird it belonged to, and how many eggs it contained. He was always the first person in the family to hear the cuckoo, and sometimes he would go alone in the evenings to watch the rabbits on the hill, an occupation which needed more patience and stillness than Paul had ever been able to muster.

After a few minutes Jo came back and squatted down beside Paul, looking once more at the footprint in the earth.

'That's not a dog,' he muttered.

'It must be,' said Paul. 'What else could it possibly be, Jo?' Jo puffed out his cheeks and looked at the sky.

'It's either a fox or a badger.'

Paul let out a hoot of laughter. 'Don't be barmy! A fox or a badger! In London!' He went on laughing while Jo, looking very offended, sat silent.

'All right, all right clever Dick,' Jo said at last, as he pushed Paul backwards on to the grass. 'If it's a dog – then what lives in the hole?' Paul looked up at the sky and blinked. 'You see,' Jo went on triumphantly, 'You can't answer that, can you?'

'Yes I can,' said Paul, suddenly sitting up. 'Rabbits.' It was just possible, he thought, that rabbits might live here; perhaps tame ones that had escaped and were living in the wild.

'It's too big for a rabbit burrow,' said Jo firmly. 'Besides there are no droppings. Have you ever seen a rabbit hole that didn't have droppings outside?'

Paul shook his head. 'But it couldn't possibly be a badger or a fox,' he objected.

'It might be,' said Jo stubbornly. 'Anyway, that fox's earth in the woods was just like this.'

Paul stood up and brushed the leaves off his legs. He was beginning to feel hungry. 'Well anyway, we'll never prove it. And we've got to go now.' He started to walk back up the hill. 'Come on, Jo,' he called over his shoulder. 'We'll be late for lunch.'

Jo followed him slowly up the slope, turning frequently to look back at the clump of bushes. No matter what Paul might say he was convinced that he was right. The more he thought about the burrow, the more sure he became that it belonged to a fox, however improbable it seemed. Under the bushes by the dip, there had been a funny smell, like old pennies. That was fox, that smell, and nothing else. But the only way to be absolutely sure, Jo knew, was to see the fox itself.

As he trudged along behind Paul, Jo went over all he knew or had ever learnt about foxes, and he discovered that he didn't know very much. What, for instance, did they eat? Everyone knew about foxes stealing chickens, but there weren't any chickens in London. Did they eat birds? Or worms? He was fairly sure that both would be easy to find, on the slope, or on the Heath itself.

At the top of the hill Paul stopped, remembering how they had launched the kite. When Jo caught up with him, he said, 'I meant it, you know. About the twenty-four pence.'

Jo frowned. 'Ssh,' he said. 'I'm thinking.' Paul shrugged his shoulders angrily and walked on. Sometimes he just didn't understand Jo at all. Surely that burrow couldn't be more important than the kite. Well anyway, he wasn't going to offer Jo his money again. He could jolly well save up himself to buy another kite.

'Thinking,' he said sourly, after there had been silence for a long time. 'Huh! You'll be thinking you've seen a dragon's lair next. Fox indeed! Huh! Big joke that, foxes in London. Very funny!'

Jo looked at him. 'What's wrong with you?' he asked mildly. 'It might be. There must be things for a fox to eat on the Heath. Mice and worms. I saw a squirrel just now.'

'Bet you didn't.'

'Yes I did. Going up a tree. Perhaps foxes eat squirrels.'

'Ugh!' Paul made a face. They had reached the iron posts and Jo stopped and turned round to look back at the Heath.

'You know,' he said slowly, 'if we came back this evening, when it's getting dark, we might see it. If it is a fox.'

44

'Oh forget it, can't you,' Paul said impatiently. 'I told you before that it was a dog. You could see by the print.'

'No,' said Jo. 'It wasn't. Anyway I'm going to find out if it is a fox. You don't have to come if you don't want to.'

'What about the kite?' Paul asked. 'You were the one who wanted to get it back in the first place.'

'Yes,' said Jo, 'I know. But it's gone now, and the burrow's still there. But I'll tell you something,' he went on fiercely, 'no one's going to spoil that. No one. That's our secret, and I bet no one else knows about it. I bet Michael Skinner and his stupid, skinny gang haven't got the sense to know a fox's earth when they see one. I bet they hardly know the difference between a cat and a dog, they're so stupid. Just breaking things and spoiling everything.'

'We don't know they've broken it.'

'Oh, I'm sure they have,' said Jo, digging at the ground with his toe.

'Well, we could get another kite – with my money,' said Paul, relenting now that he saw how upset Jo really was.

'Maybe,' said Jo. 'But I'm going back to watch that hole first. Are you coming with me or not?' Paul opened his mouth to say 'no' and then closed it again. He remembered the shed and how Jo had managed quite well without him. He wished now that he had taken part in all that painting and planning. If there *was* something in this fox idea of Jo's after all, it would be awful to be left out of that too. Besides, Paul reflected, with Michael Skinner and his gang around he and Jo had better stick together.

'Well?' Jo asked, putting his head on one side.

'OK,' Paul said. 'But I still bet you it's a dog.'

'We'll see,' Jo grinned. 'Anyway, I'm glad you're in it too. More fun than being alone.' And he leap-frogged over the iron post and raced up the street, leaving Paul to follow.

6

The First Glimpse

At the same time as Paul and Jo were making their way back up Brownlow Street and wondering whether they were late for lunch, Mr Tomlinson, several miles away in his office in the City, was beginning to think that it was time for his lunch as well.

Selling artificial fertilizers, which was Mr Tomlinson's job, is not always very interesting, and during that Friday morning he had found time to make two telephone calls, one to the Cottage Hospital, and the other to enquire about trains down to Martinford. The next day Mrs Tomlinson was going to Martinford to see her mother while Mr Tomlinson and the boys stayed in London.

Thinking about trains down to Martinford made Mr Tomlinson think about the country, and as he looked out of his office window at the grimy roofs and the people hurrying past on the pavements below, he wondered if moving to London had been the right thing to do. He was beginning to wonder whether, when his six months' trial period in the head office was over, he wouldn't ask for his old job back again. The boys hadn't settled down as well as they should have done, and he and his wife both missed the country. There were too many people and houses and not enough fresh air, he reflected. Perhaps London just didn't suit them.

'Ever been to a park called Hampstead?' he asked the typist who brought him some letters to sign.

'Ooh, Mr Tomlinson, it's easy to tell you aren't a Londoner,' she giggled.

'Is it well known?' he asked, surprised.

'I should just say it is. I was there myself last bank holiday. They have a fair, you see. Donkey rides and all. My boyfriend took me.'

When she had gone Mr Tomlinson put on his hat and went over to the café where he always had lunch, and as he went he tried to puzzle out where, exactly, the Heath could be, and why, if it was so close, neither he nor his wife had ever noticed it.

At 35 Brownlow Street, Mrs Tomlinson spooned stewed beef and carrots on to the boys' plates in an absent-minded fashion.

'I wonder how poor Granny is today,' she said as she sat down. 'Your dad said he'd telephone the hospital this morning and find out.'

'Is it bad – having a broken leg?' Paul asked.

'No-o. But when you're that age – and I don't think she's ever been in hospital before.'

'I could write to her,' said Paul. 'People like getting letters when they're ill, don't they?'

'That would be nice,' said his mother, brightening up at once. 'She'd like that. And there's no use my worrying till your father gets home and we know how she is. So after lunch I'll just go and pull some weeds out of that border at the back.'

'I'll help with that, Mum,' said Jo suddenly. 'I'm quite good at weeding.' Paul looked at Jo and wondered what he was up to; his mother was too preoccupied to notice, though she did look suspicious when Jo scraped up the last of his semolina and asked for a second helping.

'I didn't think you liked semolina,' she said. Jo opened his eyes very wide and smiled at her.

'I've changed my mind. By the way,' he added, 'after the weeding, Paul and I thought we might go back to the Heath.' Mrs Tomlinson let a huge dollop of semolina slide from the spoon into Jo's bowl while she looked at him.

'After tea, you mean?' she asked. Jo nodded. 'But it'll be getting dark by then.'

'That's all right. We know the way, don't we, Paul?' Mrs Tomlinson put the spoon down and shook her head.

'No,' she said, and shut her mouth tightly.

'Oh Mum,' Jo wailed. 'We won't get lost or anything.'

'No,' said Mrs Tomlinson again. 'And that's that. I'm not having you two wandering about London after dark, so you needn't bother to ask any more.' Jo's mouth turned down at the corners and he stared sulkily at the semolina. 'Come on now, eat that up,' his mother added. 'I want to clear the table.'

Poor Jo. Paul couldn't help smiling. He had eaten all that semolina which he hated, and had promised to help with the weeding, and now he wasn't allowed to go back to his burrow. Paul wouldn't have blamed him if he had thrown his plate through the window. But Jo wasn't like that. If he found one way blocked, then he just went on thinking until he found another way. Trying to keep Jo down was like trying to stop a rubber ball from bouncing.

But as the afternoon wore on Jo realized that he would have to give up, for today at least. Sadly he fetched his pencils and drawing block and, lying on the living-room floor, he began to draw foxes. Foxes lying down and sitting up, jumping, running, and standing on their hind legs.

'What are you drawing, Jo?' his father asked, peering down at him from the armchair in which he sat, reading the evening paper.

'Foxes,' said Jo without looking up. 'You ever seen one, Dad?'

'Once or twice.'

'I never have,' said Jo thoughtfully.

'Don't suppose you have,' his father chuckled. 'You've got to get up early in the morning to catch sight of a fox. Cunning blighters they are.' Jo's eyes suddenly brightened, and he chewed the end of his pencil thoughtfully. Without knowing it, his father had given him the answer he needed.

Jo's scheme depended upon his waking very early the next morning, but that didn't worry him since he had taught himself some time ago the trick of waking up whenever he wanted to. Before he went to bed he put out an extra sweater and laid his clothes on the end of his bed. Time enough to tell Paul about the plan in the morning, he thought as he went to sleep.

When he awoke it was still dark; he remembered at once what he had to do, and he felt under his pillow for his torch. The hands of his watch showed ten to five by the light of the torch, and he climbed out of bed and began to dress.

Paul was very deeply asleep and Jo had to shake him several times to wake him up. Paul groaned, opening his eyes, and then closing them again. 'It's still the middle of the night,' he grumbled. 'Leave me alone.'

'You'll be sorry if I do,' Jo hissed in his ear. 'The

50

burrow . . . we're going to the burrow.' At last Paul sat up.

'Now?' he asked.

'Yes. It's five o'clock.'

'OK' said Paul, really awake at last, and hauled himself out of bed.

'Extra sweater,' Jo whispered. 'It'll be cold.'

Going downstairs every step seemed to creak, and at the bottom they waited breathlessly, listening for any sound from their parents' room. But all was quiet.

In the kitchen they put on their shoes and anoraks, and Jo flashed his torch at the clock.

'We'll have to hurry,' he whispered. 'It'll be getting light soon.'

Outside it was cold. The street stretched away in front of them, deserted under the light of the orange lamps. Paul put his hand on Jo's arm.

'Do you really think we should?' he asked. 'It's still dark. I'm sure we'll get into trouble.'

'I don't see why,' Jo answered. 'Mum didn't say anything about the early morning, did she?' Paul hesitated. He didn't want to be left out. 'Of course, if you're scared,' Jo went on, 'you'd better go back.'

'I'm not scared,' said Paul.

'Well, come on then,' said Jo and set off up the street.

As they ran down the little street which led to the Heath a faint grey light was beginning to streak the blackness of the sky. But once they were on the Heath it seemed dark and mysterious; it was silent too, for even the birds were not awake yet, and Paul and Jo kept close to one another as they made their way up the hill.

They found their way easily enough to the place

where they had climbed the wall the day before, and as they clambered over Jo noticed that several lights had gone on in houses beyond the railway line. People were beginning to get up, and the dawn was lightening the sky. They were only just in time, Jo thought. A little way down the hill he laid his hand on Paul's arm.

'I'll go first now,' he whispered. 'We must be very quiet and slow, and not talk – at all.'

'OK,' Paul said.

'When we get there,' Jo went on, 'sit where I tell you and don't make a noise. And don't move either.' Paul nodded. 'We'll have to try to keep upwind,' Jo murmured.

Paul followed as he tacked down the hill towards the hollow, wondering whether Jo really remembered which clump of bushes was the right one. They all looked the same in the half light.

After a few moments Jo stopped and looked about him; then he set off again, more cautiously. He was moving slowly now, and Paul did the same, putting one foot down in front of the other with care.

They had reached a much smaller clump of bushes, above and to the right of the one under which the earth was sited. Jo looked around him crouched down behind the bushes and then stood up and beckoned to Paul to follow.

Together they squatted down so that they were partly hidden by the lower branches, but they had a good view of the clump where the burrow was, as well as a wide stretch of the bank all around them.

It was becoming lighter all the time now, and Paul could make out the features of the hillside. Jo's face, he could see, had that quiet, intent look which meant that he was listening as well as watching. Paul did his best to copy him, but it was uncomfortable behind the bush and the wet grass was soaking his trousers and making his legs feel cold and stiff. He found it difficult not to fidget, and even harder not to talk during the long silence which followed. He kept thinking of things he wanted to say; but he dared not speak.

Jo was hearing all kinds of things. There were small rustlings and flutterings in the bushes all around as the birds began to wake, and in a tree in one of the gardens above them the first thrush took up his post and began to greet the new day. Below them the trains passed from time to time, signalling the passing minutes.

Paul's knees and the backs of his legs where they were tucked under him on the wet grass were so sore by now that he was beginning to think he couldn't stand it a moment longer without moving, when he felt Jo stiffen beside him, and lay a hand on his arm.

Paul did his best to follow the direction of Jo's eyes. At first he could see nothing. Then, suddenly, he made out a dark, shadowy form moving up the rise in the direction of the large clump of bushes. It stopped. Jo tightened his grip on Paul. Any movement now would be fatal. Paul understood and, motionless, he held his breath.

It was some time before the form began to move forward again, stealthily and silently. As it approached it took on a shape, and for a moment Paul thought that it was a dog after all. He could see a long, sharp nose and two pricked ears; but there was something about the way it moved which didn't seem at all dog-like.

The fox, for a fox it was, came more swiftly up the hill now, but it was alert and uneasy and just below the burrow it stopped again, looking round. The boys were close enough to see the flick of its ears as it listened. And then they saw something else. A dark shape, like a rag, dangled from the fox's mouth.

It must have reached the entrance to the burrow now, for it sat down and they saw its head drop for a moment as it let go of the object which it was carrying. Then something else happened. Something totally unexpected. Suddenly there were two more shapes beside the fox, smaller shapes, moving quickly to merge into the one shadowy shape of the fox on the ground in front of them, and then separating out again so that there were once more three shapes.

Paul watched in astonishment, unable to make it out, and not daring to take his eyes off what was going on to look at Jo for a clue. But Paul was only puzzled for a moment. Then he smiled.

They were cubs. The fox had cubs, and once Paul realized this everything began to make sense. Through the stillness there came soft, yapping noises as the cubs ran back and forth, tussling over their breakfast and dragging it along the ground between them. The vixen lay beside them, still alert, for her head was up and her ears twitched, but resting and watching the young ones.

Then, suddenly, it ended. The fox lifted her head,

sniffed, and gave a low growl. In a moment the whole family had gone, leaving the hillside empty and quiet again. What had startled her it was impossible to tell, for everything seemed as quiet as it had been before, but she and the cubs had disappeared beneath the ground, and the boys were left alone.

'I told you,' said Jo softly, his eyes blazing with triumph and delight. 'I told you, didn't I?'

'But why did they go?' Paul asked. 'I wanted to go on watching – there were cubs, weren't there?'

'Two of them,' Jo nodded. 'Fantastic. I never expected that.' Jo stood up and rubbed his legs. 'Of course,' he went on, 'no one would ever believe us. I bet you no one else knows that there are foxes here.'

'If only we could have got closer to them,' Paul said. 'You don't suppose they're tame, do you?'

'Of course not,' said Jo scornfully. 'They're as wild as they are in the country. Anyone could see that.'

At the top of the bank they stopped. 'I suppose,' Paul said slowly, 'I mean – we couldn't have been mistaken could we?'

'I know what you mean,' Jo nodded. 'It seems impossible, doesn't it?'

'Right in the middle of London,' Paul said.

'But we *did* see them,' Jo said. 'We both did.'

They climbed over the wall and walked back to the Heath in silence. By the time they reached the iron posts Paul could tell that Jo had something he wanted to say, so he stopped.

'What's up?' he asked.

Jo was rather red. 'I've been thinking,' he began, digging the ground with his toe, 'no one's going to believe us, and Mum and Dad are sure to ask questions like when we saw the fox, and where we saw it. They'll

55

probably try to stop us from coming back . . .'

'Because it's so early in the morning you mean?' Paul broke in.

'Exactly. And early morning is just about the only time when we can come and watch. If we keep it as our secret then no one can spoil it. What do you think, Paul? Suppose we don't tell anyone?'

'No one?'

'Not a single soul. And we'll come back again the first chance we get. Go on, swear not to tell.'

'All right,' Paul said, crossing his heart, 'I swear. I want to see them again too. I wonder if we ever will, Jo?'

7

Enter Neville

Paul and Jo were not to have the opportunity of visiting the burrow again for two days. Mrs Tomlinson went to see her mother in the Cottage Hospital that Saturday, and the morning passed in a whirl of activity. Directly breakfast was over the whole family set off for the station to see her off, and if Paul and Jo felt any sadness at seeing the train pull out of the station without them, it soon melted away when their father suggested lunch in a snack bar, and a trip to the cinema afterwards.

On Sunday morning they both slept late, for they were tired out after their early start the day before. Then Mrs Tomlinson suggested they should go for a walk on the Heath. Now that she had been down to Martinford and seen for herself that her mother was getting on all right she was her old, cheerful self again; and so after lunch they all set off.

Mr and Mrs Tomlinson were almost as surprised and delighted with the Heath as Paul and Jo had been. The view from the top of the hill, they said, was just grand, with the whole of London spread out before them. They even said that they would think about the bicycles, now that they had seen for themselves what it was really like.

The only person who was not in a good humour was Paul. The Heath was thronged with people, young and old, all taking their Sunday walk, and it didn't seem like his Heath at all. There were people flying kites from the top of the hill, too, and Paul looked sadly towards the clump of bushes where Jo's kite had landed. It was then that he realized that today would be the perfect day to look inside the hide-out. There were too many people about for the gang to be there, and they just might have left behind Jo's kite. Anyway it was worth looking.

Leaving Jo and his parents on top of the hill, he ran towards the clump of bushes, and circled round it until he found a gap through which he could push his way.

He found himself in a space just large enough for him to stand upright. The ground was hard and dry, for the branches grew so thickly that little rain could get through. There was an unpleasant smell, too, which made Paul wrinkle his nose in distaste. But to his astonishment there was nothing there. Nothing at all. He had expected to find something, and he searched around for a couple of minutes; but all he discovered was a chocolate wrapper and some lolly sticks. It wasn't a hide-out at all, he thought, pushing his way out again. It was just – well – a clump of bushes.

At the back of Paul's mind all the time was the thought that sooner or later he and Jo were going to meet the gang again, and Michael Skinner was like a shadow flitting in and out of his thoughts. He knew that Michael hadn't forgotten about them, and it wasn't over. Not by any means.

On the way home Mr Tomlinson stopped opposite the dairy and admired the front gardens on each side of the road; but he was looking at the houses too. The house in Brownlow Street was let to them for only six months, and if they were going to stay in London they would have to find somewhere else to live.

'Mm. Wood End Grove,' said Mrs Tomlinson, reading the street name out loud. 'Better than Brownlow

Street anyway. Those rooms are too dark – and it's damp.'

Mr Tomlinson smiled, but he didn't say anything. There was time enough to decide about moving. The first thing they had to do was to make up their minds whether they were going to stay in London or not.

Jo went to bed that night with the intention of waking up early and going to the burrow. But when he opened his eyes the next morning he was disconcerted to find that it was broad daylight. He hoisted himself up on one elbow and looked across at Paul, who was still asleep, flat on his back with both arms above his head. As he looked at him, Paul opened his eyes and sat up.

'What time is it?'

'Too late to go now,' said Jo. 'We overslept.'

'Bother,' said Paul crossly. He yawned and climbed out of bed, padding across to the window. 'Oh well, we couldn't have gone anyway. It's been pouring with rain and it looks as though it's only just stopped. There are puddles all over the path.'

'That's why I overslept,' said Jo. 'I always do on wet days.'

'It doesn't matter. We can go to the Heath anyway, and go back to the burrow tomorrow.' He stretched and yawned again. It felt like a good day anyhow, Paul thought.

It was the Heath that had made days seem like proper days again, and not like prison sentences – down the hill to school and then up the hill again from school and back home. The knowledge that all that open space was just a short walk away had changed everything.

After breakfast they went out. It was damp, with a soft wind blowing from the west and the rain was holding off, but only just. Jo said that he wanted to go to the

59

sweet shop on the way, and Paul, exploring in his anorak pocket found that he had a shilling. Jo bought shrimps as usual, but Paul decided to have a whole bar of chocolate. It wasn't every day he found a shilling he had forgotten about.

Outside the shop a boy was leaning against the railings. He was short and dumpy, with a pale face and glasses, and he looked as though he was waiting for them. Paul recognized him and nudged Jo.

'Come on,' he said, 'let's get going,' and he set off down the hill before the boy could say anything.

Jo was dawdling as usual, counting his shrimps.

''Lo,' said the boy, coming towards him. 'I seen you before.'

'Yes,' said Jo, glancing up, 'at school.'

'I live in your street too.'

'What number?' Jo asked politely.

'Twenty-five.'

'We're thirty-five. Want a shrimp?'

'Come *on*, Jo,' Paul called.

'That your brother?' asked the boy.

'Yes. He's Paul and I'm Jo. I've forgotten your name.'

'Neville,' said the boy. 'Where are you going?'

'To the Heath,' Jo said.

'I'm going without you,' Paul shouted, walking backwards down the hill so that he could keep going and watch at the same time.

'Got to go now,' said Jo. 'See you.'

At that moment Paul walked backwards into a woman with a push-chair and fell over, upsetting her shopping basket and scattering the shopping all over the pavement. When Jo reached them Paul was apologizing and picking up the bags of sugar and sausages, and the baby in the push-chair was howling. By the time the

60

woman had soothed the baby and Paul and Jo had put all the shopping back in the basket, Neville had caught up and was standing beside them staring owlishly through his glasses at what was going on.

'Well, what do you want?' Paul asked crossly.

'I know a quicker way to the Heath than that. I'll show you if you like. It's over the railway bridge. Brings you out by the playground,' Neville explained.

All the way to the bridge Paul kept trying to tell Jo that Neville was one of Michael Skinner's gang, but Jo didn't seem to notice his signals. Paul thought that they might be walking into a trap, and he kept a sharp look out for other members of the gang. But there didn't seem to be any boys about except themselves, only women with shopping bags and smaller kids.

The bridge was wide, flanked on either side by a high metal parapet so that it was impossible to see the trains without hoisting oneself up. Along one side of the parapet someone had written 'PAT LOVES LUCY' in red paint. The paint had run and left a long dripping line under each letter which looked like blood.

The bridge made Paul feel creepy and he wanted to get across it and out on to the Heath. But Jo and Neville were trying to climb the parapet so that they could look at the trains below. When Paul tried to do it too he found that it was difficult. There was nowhere on the smooth surface where his feet could get a grip, and once up there he had to rest all the weight of his body on his arms to prevent himself from slipping back.

Down below the line ran towards a tunnel. The signals were up which meant that a train was due, and farther back down the line behind them, they could hear it.

'Bet you can't stay up here till it's gone under the bridge,' Neville gasped.

'Bet I can,' said Paul, but his arms were already aching and it seemed hours before the engine appeared below them, pulling a long line of goods wagons behind it.

Neville was the first to slip down off the parapet. 'Whew!' He pushed his glasses back up his nose. 'That was close. I thought it was never coming.'

Where the Heath began was a playground with swings and seesaws which Paul remembered noticing from the top of the hill.

'You coming in there?' Neville asked, edging close to Paul and looking at him curiously through his glasses. Paul shook his head and moved a step backwards in aversion. He was certain now that Neville was one of the gang. He remembered seeing him with the others in the playground last term. He was beginning, also, to have the feeling that Neville had been sent to spy on them. He looked round to see if Jo was coming. Jo had been the last to slip down from the parapet and he was walking slowly across the bridge.

Neville pulled up his socks and stood looking at Paul. 'It's great in there,' he said persuasively.

'Actually,' Paul said, 'we're going to look for Jo's kite. Some boys stole it a couple of days ago.' Neville's mouth came open and he backed away quickly.

'See you then,' he muttered and moved off in the direction of the playground. Paul grinned.

'He went quickly,' said Jo, catching up with Paul. 'What did you say to him?'

'Nothing much,' said Paul, looking over his shoulder. Neville was standing by the railings which surrounded the playground, staring at them. 'We didn't want him hanging round, did we? I kept trying to tell you, he's one of Michael Skinner's gang.'

'Are you sure?'

Paul nodded. 'And I think he's spying on us too.'

Jo stared at Paul in dismay. 'We'll have to shake him off,' he said. 'Is he still watching us?'

'I can't see him.'

'We'd better get to the top of the hill and then look again,' said Jo. 'Something's happened. Something important.'

'What?' Paul asked. Jo looked very solemn.

'I don't suppose you saw, when we were looking over the bridge back there. You never see anything, do you?'

'Well, what was it?' Paul asked impatiently.

'Down beside the line ... It looked like a fox. It was the right colour. I looked at it for quite a long time. It might have been a ginger cat, I suppose.' Jo was talking to himself as much as to Paul.

'But it couldn't have been the fox,' Paul interrupted. 'Not at this time of day.' They were half way up the hill now. Jo stopped and looked at him for a moment in silence. Then he shouted very loudly.

'You stupid mug! It was dead. Whatever it was, it was DEAD.'

'Dead?'

'Yes,' said Jo more quietly. 'Quite dead. It must have trodden on a live rail.'

'Are you sure?' Paul couldn't really believe it.

'No. Not sure.' Jo shook his head. 'But whatever it was we've got to find out, and we can't have Neville hanging round.'

They had reached the top of the hill now; the ground swept away down the hill, uninterrupted by bushes or trees, a huge, rather muddy expanse of grass. It was easy for Paul and Jo to see Neville's solitary figure sitting on a swing in the playground. They could even see the white blur of his face as he turned to look up the hill.

'You were right,' said Jo. 'He's obviously watching us. What are we going to do?'

'There,' said Paul. 'We'll move over there.'

Crouching behind a hawthorn bush they saw him stand up and gaze towards the hill, trying to see where they had gone, but although he walked over to the railings and scanned the hillside, he didn't leave the playground. After a few moments he looked over his shoulder towards the bridge and back up the hill again. Paul slapped his knee.

'Got it!' he said.

'He's waiting for the gang. That's why he keeps looking round – to see if they're coming. He's been told to wait for them there, and probably to keep us there too. That's why he wanted to get us into the playground. I knew it was a trap.'

'Well, come on then,' said Jo urgently. 'Let's get going before the others arrive.'

They ran across the path which lay along the top of the hill, and down the other side, out of sight of the playground and Neville. Where the ground flattened out they began to move to the left, towards the perimeter of the Heath, making for the cover of the bushes.

'I think we've made it,' Jo gasped, as they worked their way along beside a high, brick wall. They had almost reached the street.

'Wait a moment,' Paul hissed. 'Get down.' But it was only a crowd of girls going past. 'I think it's safe now,' said Paul. 'Let's go!'

As they ran up the street they kept looking round, but there was no one following them, and the street was deserted.

At the wall they stopped for breath.

'What now?' Paul asked.

'Down to the line,' said Jo grimly. 'We should be able to get a good look at whatever it is from down there.'

They made their way down the hill until they reached the fence which divided the bank from the railway line, and then began to work their way back towards the bridge. It seemed to take ages, for the going was rough and the grass long and over-grown.

At last Jo said, 'There's the bridge,' and they slowed down, looking more carefully beyond the fence where the live rails began.

'How much farther?' Paul asked.

'It must be near here,' Jo muttered. Then they saw it, just beyond the fence. At first it looked like an old brown coat someone had thrown away, but as they came closer they saw the shape of the fox clearly. Its head was thrown back, it mouth wide open, and its eyes glazed. There was no doubt about it. The fox was dead. They stared for a moment until, unable to look any longer, Paul turned away and gazed up the hill.

'Well that's that,' he said.

8

The Rescue

Paul began to walk away at once, without waiting for Jo. Just at that moment he couldn't bear to see Jo's face. He knew how much the fox had meant to him, and now, like the kite the other day, everything was ruined. He looked around him at the damp grass and the damp grey sky and wondered miserably why everything had to end up like this.

'Where are you going?' Jo asked, catching up with him. Paul shrugged, looking at the ground. 'You can't go yet,' Jo said urgently. 'What about the cubs?'

Paul spun round and stared at Jo. The cubs. Of course. He had forgotten about the cubs. The fox was dead, but the cubs might still be alive, and if they were . . . Paul let out a low whistle.

'Come on,' said Jo. 'We'd better go and look.'

When they reached the clump of bushes, Jo stopped and crouched down, signalling Paul to do the same. For a while they were silent, huddled together on the wet grass, watching the entrance to the burrow. There was no sign of movement; the minutes passed and nothing happened.

'It's no good,' Paul whispered.

'Hang on,' Jo answered. 'We've hardly been here any time yet.' It was very quiet. Even the birds were silent this morning, huddled in the branches of the trees against the rain which would soon begin to fall once more.

Jo was beginning to give up hope when, suddenly, he was aware that the entrance to the burrow was no longer a dark, vacant hole in the hillside. There was a movement in the centre of the darkness, and the next moment a small head appeared. He could make out two pricked ears; then there were four ears, and the next moment both cubs were squeezing themselves out of the burrow to sit on the grass, just a few paces from where Paul and Jo were sitting.

The boys watched, motionless, almost afraid to breathe. Now that it was daylight it was easier to see what the cubs really looked like. They were still very babyish, more like puppies than fox cubs. Their ears, which later would be large and pointed were small and soft and their tails were small too, tapering off at the end, and not at all like the magnificent full brush of the adult fox. They were covered with soft, brown fur and they both had white chests; one of them also had a white tip to its tail.

After a moment the cubs began to move about, sniffing the ground, and occasionally looking up as though they were listening for something. They didn't move very far from the entrance to the burrow, but they didn't seem to be afraid. When a blackbird suddenly flew up into a tall tree behind them, squawking noisily, the cubs looked round, ears pricked, watching the way it had gone. Then, after a moment they resumed their sniffing.

When they had seen the fox dead beside the line, Jo had wondered whether it was, in fact, their fox. It might have been another one, for he and Paul had no idea how many foxes there were living along the bank. Now that the cubs had come out from the burrow, however, he was certain that the dead fox was the vixen they had seen the other morning. The cubs were still too young, Jo guessed, to leave the burrow without good reason, and in broad daylight. It was clear that they were looking for the vixen.

Just then the smaller of the two cubs, the one with the white tip to its tail, suddenly sat down. It looked as though its legs had collapsed under it, and a small whine escaped from it. The second cub looked at it and uttered a sharp, thin bark. They were the most pathetic sounds Jo had ever heard, and in that moment he decided what had to be done.

He didn't know how long the vixen had been lying dead on the railway line below them. Perhaps since Saturday night, because the cubs were clearly very hungry. If they didn't have food soon, Jo thought, they would die. Without wondering how he was going to catch them, and without saying anything to Paul, Jo began to move out from behind the bush.

He went very slowly and cautiously on all fours. The cubs were looking down the hill, sitting close together, watching as though the vixen might appear at any moment, wending her way up the slope towards them as she had done so many times before. So absorbed were the small creatures that Jo managed to get clear of the bush before they turned and saw him. He stopped at once.

They looked at him curiously with their small, bright eyes, but neither of them moved. Jo didn't move either, and after a moment they looked away from him again, back down the hillside. Jo waited, and then moved forward once more.

This time they watched his approach. He moved steadily but slowly until he was close enough to touch them with an outstretched arm, and it was only then

69

that the larger of the two cubs backed away a few paces and gave a low growl. Jo stopped and sat up on the grass quite still, waiting to see what they would do next.

Behind the bush Paul crouched breathlessly, expecting at any moment that the cubs would take fright and bolt into the burrow. But they only shifted a little, settling themselves into their new position, and watched Jo uneasily, dividing their attention between him and the hill.

It was then that Paul had an idea of his own. He had seen at once that Jo intended to catch the cubs. Now he thought of a way to help, and fishing in his pocket he pulled out the chocolate he had bought earlier that morning. The meeting with Neville had made him forget it until now, which was just as well or by this time he would have eaten it.

Every animal Paul had ever known had liked chocolate. Obviously, he thought, the cubs would like it too, and without waiting any longer he began to wriggle out from behind the bush and across the grass towards Jo.

The cubs saw him at once and they stiffened. Paul knew that if he moved too quickly and they took fright and ran back to the burrow, Jo would never forgive him, and he felt his heart begin to thump with anxiety. But the cubs didn't run, and Paul kept going.

Jo must have heard him coming, but he sat like a rock as Paul slithered across the grass towards him. When at last Paul was close enough to Jo for him to see it, he held up the chocolate without speaking. Jo's face lit up and he nodded.

Paul slipped off the paper wrapper and turned back the silver paper. He knew just what he was going to do. First he would throw a piece almost to the cubs' feet, and then, as they ate it and became bolder, he would shorten the distance between each throw until they were within reach.

He threw the first piece gently across the space separating him from the cubs. The sudden movement made them flinch, and they backed away. Then the larger of the two began nosing in the grass. Paul held his breath. Perhaps it wouldn't work. Perhaps fox cubs didn't like chocolate after all.

Then the cub pushed the chocolate with its nose. Seeing that it didn't bite, and as it smelt good to eat, it licked the chocolate experimentally. The next moment the cub was sitting looking expectantly towards Paul and licking its lips, and the smaller cub was sniffing the grass.

Paul looked at Jo triumphantly and broke off two more pieces which he tossed towards the cubs, but a little closer this time, so that they had to move towards

71

him. There was a sudden scramble, a whirl of tails and a jabbing of noses and then both cubs were looking at him again.

'Closer next time,' Jo breathed.

Four pieces of chocolate later the cubs were at Paul's feet. Any sudden movement made them start backwards, but their eyes were bright with hunger, and Paul and Jo knew that they had won.

After that catching them was easy. One moment the cubs were standing on the grass looking at Paul, and the next moment Jo was holding one and Paul the other. They wriggled and bit at first, but they were so hungry that the offer of more chocolate quietened them at once, and Paul and Jo, each hugging a cub, stared at one another with a mixture of astonishment and delight. For a few moments Paul and Jo forgot about the wet grass and the dead vixen on the line below them. They even forgot that the cubs were hungry and probably cold as well. It was enough just to hold them, to stroke their soft, brown fur and look into their small, inquisitive faces.

The rain, which had been threatening all morning, began to fall at last, and Jo scrambled to his feet, clutching his cub more tightly to his chest.

'We'll have to go,' he said.

'Where to?' Paul asked.

Whatever happened to the cubs now, Jo thought, as he looked around him at the hillside, they wouldn't be his secret and Paul's any more. The grown-ups would take over, and that would be that. He supposed that they would have to be taken to some zoo or something. He wrapped his anorak around the cub to keep it dry and warm and then, turning his back on the wet hillside he began to climb towards the wall.

'What's the matter, Jo?' asked Paul, sensing the change in Jo's mood. 'You're not cross because it was my idea about the chocolate are you?' Jo shook his head. 'What then?'

Jo stroked the cub's ears in silence for a moment. 'We'll have to take them home and tell Mum now. And then they'll be taken away from us. We'll never see them again.'

'Still, we have saved them from starving to death, Jo.'

'I know. I just don't want it to end, that's all.'

'Mine's gone very quiet,' said Paul, peering down inside his anorak. 'Do you think they're weak with hunger?'

When they reached the Heath, Paul and Jo turned towards the hill, leaving the playground and the railway bridge behind them. They couldn't risk running into Neville or the rest of the gang, although it would have been quicker to go that way.

The Heath looked bleak under the rain, which was falling now with a steady insistence. Before long the ends of their trouser legs were soaked through and the water had begun to drip down inside their shoes. But underneath their anoraks the cubs were warm and dry, and the gentle jogging movement of the walking soothed them, whilst the warmth of the boys' bodies revived them.

'Ugh!' said Paul. 'This rotten rain.' With every step the weight of the cub inside his jacket seemed to become greater. 'You wouldn't think they'd be so heavy, would you? And mine keeps slipping down.'

'We'll stop when we get to the posts,' said Jo.

It wasn't only the rain, or the weight of the cub inside his jacket which made Jo silent. He was working out a plan, and when they reached the posts and stopped for

73

a moment, resting their weight against the metal and shifting the cubs round inside their jackets, he was ready to tell Paul about it.

'I've been thinking,' he said. 'We don't have to tell Mum about the cubs yet.'

'We can't possibly keep them a secret,' said Paul, wiping the rain from his forehead with his free hand.

'Yes, we can. I've thought of the perfect place to hide them.'

'Where? Not in our room.'

'They'd be found there, stupid.'

'Where then?'

Jo put his head on one side and looked at Paul. 'Somewhere no one ever goes except us. Somewhere quite safe, and dry. AND somewhere with a lock and key. My shed,' he finished with a grin. 'My shed, of course.'

9

Neville the Spy

Paul unhitched himself from the post. This time, he thought, Jo had gone too far.

'We can't do it,' he said, shaking his head.

'Why not?' Jo wanted to know.

'We can't, that's all.'

'But why not? You haven't said why not?'

'Well, for a start,' Paul said, 'what would we feed them on?'

'You see! I knew you'd say that,' Jo burst in, 'because it's the first thing I thought of. And I've thought of an answer too. We'll give them bread and milk first, as soon as we get home, and then,' he rushed on before Paul could interrupt, 'then we'll find out what other things they should have.'

'There you are,' said Paul. 'How are we going to find out without asking someone? And who can we ask except Mum? Can't you see it's hopeless, Jo?'

Without waiting for Jo to answer, Paul walked on. The rest beside the posts had woken his cub and it was wriggling about inside his anorak, struggling to be free. Paul felt that any moment it might jump out, and he wanted to get home as quickly as possible so that he could put the cub down somewhere safe and stretch his aching arms. He wanted to take his wet shoes off too, and as he walked along he became more and more aware of the bottoms of his trouser legs, which were now sopping wet and flapping coldly around his ankles with every step he took.

He looked round to see if Jo was following, and saw that he was walking a few paces behind him and looking the very picture of dejection. It wasn't his fault, Paul thought. It was crazy of Jo to think that they could keep the cubs a secret. At Martinford where there were more places to hide things they might have been able to do it. But in London it was hopeless. Anyhow, Jo didn't know for sure that they wouldn't be allowed to keep the cubs. Their mother might be quite pleased about it. Jo didn't *know* that she wouldn't be pleased.

They walked over the pedestrian crossing and turned into Brownlow Street and Jo quickened his pace until he was level with Paul. 'Paul,' he pleaded. 'Please.' Paul didn't answer. 'Couldn't we just try it? Then we could see if it's going to be too difficult.'

'What's the point,' said Paul. 'Oh come on, Jo. I want to get home.'

'Please,' said Jo plaintively. Paul sighed and leant against someone's front wall, looking at Jo. The rain was stopping at last; he eased the cub farther up, under his chin, and held it with one arm while he stretched the other one.

'You must know it's not going to be any good,' he said soberly.

Jo stuck out his lower lip. 'I don't see why not,' he said. 'The longer we can keep it a secret the more chance we have of keeping them in the end.'

'But we might be allowed to keep them anyway.'

'My way's better though. We can say that we've managed to look after them, so why can't we keep them.' Paul considered this. It would be marvellous to have the fox cubs for pets, and he could see Jo's point. Perhaps

76

if it was only for a short time, only until tomorrow, it would be all right to keep it a secret. Jo was sitting on the wall watching him anxiously.

'Do you promise to tell as soon as things get too difficult?' Paul asked at last. Jo nodded. 'All right,' Paul said. 'But I warn you we shan't be able to keep it up for long. Not more than a day.'

'We might,' said Jo, pushing his hand inside his anorak and stroking the cub's head. 'You never believe in things working, do you? You didn't believe it this morning when I said it was dead on the line – did you?'

'That was different,' Paul protested. 'Anyway, it was me that had the idea about the chocolate.'

'That was good,' Jo nodded. 'I don't suppose we'd have caught them without that.'

All this time they had been sitting on Neville's garden wall. Neville had hurried home from the Heath when the rain began without waiting any longer for the gang, and when he looked out of the front window of his house and saw Paul and Jo sitting on the wall he smiled, because he could hardly believe his luck. They had managed to shake him off earlier, but they wouldn't find it so easy now. It looked, too, as though they were up to something. Something he might be able to report to Michael.

He crept out of the house and down the garden path so stealthily that Paul and Jo didn't hear him until he was right behind them and peering over their shoulders.

'Hello,' he said. 'What you got there?' The boys both jumped and scrambled off the wall.

'What are you doing here?' Jo gasped.

Neville smiled and jerked his head at the house. 'Number 25,' he said. 'I told you.'

'Oh,' said Paul, making vain attempts to push the

cub farther down inside his jacket. 'Well, we've got to go now. Lunch.'

'Wait a sec,' said Neville, climbing onto the wall. 'What you got in there?'

'Shopping,' said Jo quickly, moving backwards so that Neville couldn't see.

'Yah! That's not shopping. It's moving.' It was true. There were frantic scrambles and small squeaks from inside Jo's anorak. 'Is it a kitten?'

'No,' said Jo hastily. Neville jumped off the wall.

'What is it then?' His glance moved over to Paul. 'Is it two kittens?' He smiled and pushed his glasses up his nose with one finger. 'Go on, tell us,' he wheedled. 'I won't split if it's a secret.'

'It's not a secret, it's shopping, and anyway mind your own business,' Paul said angrily. 'Come on, Jo. We'll be late.' Neville followed them down the street, trying all the time to peer inside their anoraks.

'Go on,' he said. 'I won't tell anyone.'

'Oh, go and jump in the lake!'

'Yes. Shove off,' Jo added. 'Off a wall.' They giggled. Neville stopped and waited until they had gone on a few paces.

'I know where your kite is,' he called after them. Paul and Jo both turned round.

'He's lying,' Paul muttered.

'Where?' Jo called back.

'I'll tell you – if you tell me what you've got in there.'

'We've already told you. Shopping,' said Jo. Neville looked at them for a moment and then shrugged. 'I'll find out anyway,' he called. 'I'll tell Michael Skinner. You wait and see.'

'Yah boo!' said Jo and stuck his tongue out. But Paul was suddenly fearful. Neville on his own was one thing; Neville backed by Michael Skinner's gang was something different.

'Oh come on, Jo,' he said. 'We don't want any trouble.'

They cut quickly down the side path that led to their back gate leaving Neville staring after them. Luckily the gate was open. Once inside they shot the bolts with relief, knowing that no one could follow them.

'I've got the key of the shed in my pocket,' said Jo. 'You'll have to hold my cub though while I go and open the door.'

'Well, don't be long,' Paul said, taking the small struggling creature from Jo.

Paul waited, crouched into the side of the house, until Jo beckoned; then he sprinted across the strip of grass and dived inside the shed.

'There,' said Jo, shutting the door firmly behind him. 'I told you it would be all right.'

'Whew!' said Paul, putting the cubs down on the ground. 'I thought we'd never make it.'

The cubs made for the darkest corner of the shed and crouched in the shadows.

'They're hungry,' said Jo. 'You stay and watch them

while I go and get the bread and milk.' Paul nodded, rubbing his arms.

Fortunately for Jo his mother had just gone upstairs with a large pile of ironing, and the kitchen was empty. He took two pieces of sliced bread and a small jug of milk from the cupboard and then looked around for something to put the mixture into. There was a plate beside the oven, but it had a bone on it. It was a shallow soup plate, just the right shape, Jo thought. He took it, bone and all, and slipped out of the back door again and down the garden path.

The cubs watched from their corner while Paul and Jo crumbled the bread and poured the milk over it, making a good sloppy mixture. Jo thought that they must be thirsty as well as hungry, and anyway at the moment milk was their natural food. The cubs kept their distance but they were obviously curious, and they stood, with legs splayed out, ears back and noses extended, sniffing the sweet smell of the milk. When the dish was ready Jo pushed it towards them, and he and Paul retired to the other corner of the shed to watch.

Slowly and warily the cubs came out of their corner and approached the plate. It was not long, however, before hunger triumphed over caution and Paul and Jo were rewarded by the gentle sound of lapping. It was only when all the milk had gone that they began to eat the bread, gobbling it down as fast as they could and not stopping until the dish was polished quite clean. Then they backed away and sat down to search for the last delicious crumbs around their whiskers.

'Well, that was all right,' Jo grinned.

'Let's give them the rest of the milk,' Paul said, tipping it into their dish.

'I brought a mutton bone too,' Jo said, 'but I think

we'd better keep that till after lunch.'

It was hard to leave the cubs, but Paul and Jo were beginning to feel cold after their walk in the rain. They made a hasty, improvised bed with some old newspapers and Jo's strip of carpet, and lifted the cubs on to it. It seemed as though the little foxes might go to sleep for they curled up, close to one another, nose to tail so that it was hard to see where one cub ended and the other began.

'They'll be all right till we get back,' Jo said.

Paul nodded, 'I'm frozen through,' he said, his teeth beginning to chatter. 'Let's go.'

Two heads came up as the boys made for the door, and four bright eyes regarded them curiously, but without fear, as they slipped out.

'Remember,' Jo said as he locked the door and put the key in his pocket. 'Not a word to Mum.'

'Not a word,' Paul nodded in agreement.

10

Jo Meets the Gang

When Mrs Tomlinson saw Paul and Jo she was not pleased. 'You're wet through, both of you, soaked to the skin,' she said. 'You'll catch your deaths of cold, and who's going to look after you then, I'd like to know.'

She made them change all their clothes, right down to vests and pants, and then wanted to know who had been in and left wet, muddy footprints all over the kitchen floor just after she'd washed it. The boys put up with it all as well as they could, Paul bearing the main brunt as usual. When there was trouble Jo had a way of becoming more and more silent until it all blew over, and when everything was calm again, up he would bob, bright as a button. It wasn't until half way through lunch that Jo judged it safe to slide back into the conversation on this occasion.

'I wonder,' he said, 'what foxes eat.'

'Foxes?' asked his mother looking at him in surprise. 'Well, they eat chickens, don't they?'

'What about baby foxes though,' Jo went on, ignoring Paul's sharp kick under the table.

'The things you boys ask,' Mrs Tomlinson said, shaking her head. 'I don't know I'm sure ...'

'Suppose you wanted to know very badly – how do you think you'd find out?' Jo persisted, chasing a plum stone round his plate.

'Well, I suppose you'd have to ask someone who did

know – or look it up in a book,' said his mother. She was thinking that in spite of the soaking they had had that morning they both looked very well, and there was more colour in Paul's cheeks than there had been for weeks, so her mind was only half on what Jo was saying.

Jo ate the rest of his lunch without another word and then pushed back his chair. 'You coming, Paul?' he asked.

'Now just a moment you two,' Mrs Tomlinson said, sensing that something was going on. 'Where are you off to?'

'Only out to the shed,' said Jo.

'You're not going back to that Heath again today.'

'No Mum, we don't want to,' Paul said, joining Jo by the back door.

'Can we go now?' Jo asked. It sounded innocent enough, Mrs Tomlinson thought. There wasn't much they could get up to in the shed.

'All right,' she said. 'Off you go.'

Jo opened the shed door cautiously and peered round. The cubs were still asleep where he and Paul had left them before lunch. He went across to them and bent down. It was a relief to see the slight rise and fall of their bodies, because for one dreadful moment Jo had thought they might be dead.

'They must be tired out,' he said quietly to Paul.

Paul had been thinking things over during lunch, and the more he thought, the more unhappy he became about keeping the secret. There seemed to be so many difficulties. There was food for a start. He didn't know, and Jo didn't know either, what fox cubs should be fed on. He remembered that there was a boy at Martinford who had kept a baby owl as a pet, and that had to be fed on cut up feathers with its meat, otherwise it would have died. There might be something like that with fox cubs too. And that wasn't the only thing. There were Neville and Michael Skinner to think about. Paul felt sure that it wouldn't be long now before Michael Skinner was round, watching to see what was going on and probably trying to wreck everything as well.

'But I don't see what they could do,' Jo objected when Paul tried to explain to him.

'But if they found out . . .'

'They won't unless one of us tells them,' Jo said. 'Neville thought they were kittens this morning. He'd never think of fox cubs. You're just making a fuss like you did about the kite – going on and on.' Paul coloured. He was sure that he was right about the gang; he felt it in his bones. But perhaps it was a thing which one just couldn't explain. Jo certainly didn't seem to understand.

'What about the food then?' he asked after a pause.

'I've had a great idea about that,' said Jo, becoming excited. 'It was Mum who gave me the idea actually . . .'

'You were daft to keep talking about foxes,' Paul interrupted. 'She might have guessed.'

'She'd never guess,' Jo said scornfully. 'Anyway, this is my idea. We can go to the library and look up foxes in a book. There's sure to be one there about them.'

'But we don't know where the library is.'

'I do. It's down by the school. We went there last term for a lecture.'

Paul went on raising objections. The library might be closed, he said. They had promised their mother they wouldn't go out. What would happen if they met the gang? Jo tried to be patient, but in the end he lost his temper.

'All right,' he hissed, standing up. 'You can jolly well

stay here and *I'll* go. If you tell Mum while I'm gone I'll bash you up – and I mean that. All you can think about it that rotten gang. I think you're just scared of them. You're just chicken, that's all.' The next moment he had gone and Paul heard the back gate slam behind him.

Paul went on sitting in the corner after Jo had gone, trying to soothe his hurt pride. He hated to be called a coward, particularly by Jo, and the worst thing about it was that deep down he felt it might be true. He had never been much of a fighter, and he disliked trouble of any kind. Even the other day when the gang had taken the kite, he remembered, Jo had been the first one to give chase. He had done nothing.

The slamming of the back gate had woken the cubs and they stretched and yawned and began to move about. They climbed down from their nest and soon they were exploring the shed, and everything in it, including Paul.

In watching their play Paul forgot his own troubles, for all his attention was on the cubs. Tails lashing in mock fury, they crouched to spring at one another, growling deep in their throats with pretended fierceness. The larger of the two, the one with the white tip to its tail, was the first to spring, and succeeded in straddling the other, biting its ears and neck. The smaller cub struggled and growled and made desperate efforts to free itself. When at last it succeeded a frantic chase round and round the shed followed, and eventually both cubs landed in a heap at Paul's feet.

When Paul put out his hand to touch them, he was surprised and delighted to find that they showed no fear at all, and allowed him to stroke them. Paul found an old piece of cloth which he knotted at one end and dragged along the ground. The cubs responded at once, and crouched down, watching the flicking movement of the cloth as Paul moved it from side to side. When the cub with the white-tipped tail caught hold of one end of the cloth, the other cub pounced on the other end, and they pulled it between them in a tug of war, growling and lashing their tails more fiercely than ever.

Down the hill in the library Jo was getting on well. The librarian had found him a book on British mammals, and he was sitting at a table, the book propped up in front of him. It took him some time to find the section on foxes, and when he did he had to wade through a great deal about their earths, and how they lived and hunted before he reached any mention of cubs. At last he read:

> The vixen usually stays with the cubs, feeding them and bringing them food for about six to eight weeks. After that the cubs begin to hunt on their own. Foxes eat small animals, such as mice, field voles and birds, but they also eat fruit sometimes and grass as well.

Jo frowned and shut the book. He guessed that the cubs might be about six weeks old, but it was only a guess. If he was right, they should probably be eating meat as well as milk. Raw meat, cut up very small. He put the book back on the shelf, thanked the librarian and went out into the street again.

On the other side of the road there was a butcher's shop. Jo crossed over and looked through the window at the meat, which was laid out in trays. It all seemed very expensive, and Jo only had twelve and a half pence. He pulled the money out of his pocket and clicked it down on the counter where the butcher could see it.

'I want some meat for the dog,' he said. The butcher looked from Jo to the coins and back to Jo again. Then he nodded and went to the window. He came back with a tray which he held over the counter for Jo to see. The meat was in long, stringy pieces, very bloody. It looked like innards, and Jo decided that the cubs might not like it. Besides it would be difficult to cut up. He shook his head. 'I don't think our dog likes that much.'

'Pernickety, eh?' said the butcher and a trace of a smile appeared on his lugubrious face. He fetched another tray. 'This?' he asked, leaning over the counter. This time the meat looked more like uncooked stew. There wasn't so much blood and it was cut into neat squares.

'Yes,' Jo nodded. He watched anxiously to see how much the butcher would put on the paper, and was glad to see that it was probably enough for two days.

Outside he raced along, dodging the shoppers and anxious to reach home. He was ready to make it up with Paul now and he wondered whether the cubs had woken yet and what they were doing.

He was half way down Brownlow Street before he saw the gang. They were lounging around Neville's front gate, and Jo could see that they were all there. He counted eight of them, with Michael Skinner in the middle. Jo swallowed hard, but he didn't stop. Paul might be scared of them, but he jolly well wasn't, and he intended to show them so.

Neville, standing on the edge of the group, was the first to see him.

'There's one of them,' Jo heard him say. He kept walking, but knew that they were all staring at him. He was past them when he heard Michael Skinner's voice.

'Hi! You!' Jo pretended he hadn't heard and walked on.

There was a sound of running feet behind him, and Michael Skinner planted himself firmly in front of Jo, blocking his path. Jo could just see, beyond Michael's left shoulder, the last house in the street. His house.

'What d'you want?' Jo asked, tilting his chin up. Michael Skinner narrowed his eyes and looked Jo up and down in silence. The others were behind him now. Foolishly, Jo tried to slide the parcel of meat behind his back, and one of the other boys saw at once what he was doing.

'What's that?' he asked, jerking his thumb at the parcel.

'Dog meat,' said Jo. 'Do you mind. I have to go now.'

'He has to go,' mocked a voice from among the crowd. 'He'll be late for tea ... late for tea ... late for tea.' The chorus ran on. Michael flipped his hand casually to silence them, but he didn't take his eyes off Jo's face.

'What did you have under your jacket this morning?' he asked.

'Mind your own business,' Jo said bravely. 'Anyway, we told your sneaky little spy – shopping.'

'Shopping doesn't squeak, does it?' Michael moved closer to Jo as he spoke. 'So what was it?'

Jo, wishing that Paul was with him, remained silent.

'Well, if you're not going to tell us, we'll just have to take that meat away, won't we?' Michael said softly. Jo grasped the precious parcel more firmly and looked at the dark sullen face of the boy in front of him.

'Why can't you leave us alone?' he asked desperately. 'You've already had my kite. Why do you have to spoil things all the time? Why?' For a moment Michael looked away from Jo and shrugged his shoulders. Then, from the back of the group of boys there came a solitary voice.

'Get the meat!'

'Yeah!' The chorus began again. 'Get the meat. Then he'll tell us.' Suddenly Jo found that he was surrounded by a circle of boys and there was no hope of escape. In that moment there flashed into his mind the memory of a hunt he had once seen. All those horses and men and hounds had streaked across the ploughed fields, filling the air with their din, and out ahead, running for its life had been the little red fox. Jo knew now what that fox must have felt like when the huntsmen began to close in. He was scared, but his chin went up in defiance and he looked round at them.

'You're just a lot of sneaky, rotten, bullying THIEVES!' he shouted.

That did it. Michael Skinner's eyes blazed and he made a dive for Jo, grabbing at the parcel. But Jo held on. In a moment he was on the ground and Michael Skinner was sitting on top of him. Jo kept fighting. He felt one or two good kicks of his go home, and he managed to hold on to the meat until someone sat on his legs and Michael began to tug at the parcel. As Michael pulled, and Jo held on, the bigger boy's hands came closer and closer towards Jo's teeth and he knew that he would be able to bite Michael's hand if he could only hold on long enough. He leant forward. Just an inch more. With a final effort he felt his teeth sink in, and heard a yell of pain.

But Michael didn't let go. The meat was slipping, slipping from Jo's grasp. In another moment the parcel would be out of his hands. Jo gritted his teeth ...

The burly man in braces who had been sitting by his window reading the newspaper decided, at that moment, that he had had enough. He threw the paper on the floor and looked out at the crowd of yelling boys in the street; then he lumbered towards his front door.

'Go on,' he shouted, as he came down the path. 'Out of it. The lot of you. Or I'll call the police.'

The gang started to back away slowly as the man advanced. They were waiting for Michael to tell them what to do.

'Go on. Out of it, I said,' the man shouted. Michael gave a last, desperate pull at the meat. Then, looking up and seeing the others disappearing down the road, he scrambled to his feet, and leaving Jo lying on the ground he followed them.

Jo rolled over and groaned. 'You too,' said the man harshly. 'And don't come back,' he called after the gang who had collected farther down the street.

With an effort Jo staggered to his feet and hobbled down the road towards Number 35. He felt sore all over, but the meat was still under his arm, and for the time being at least, he had won.

The burly man watched Jo disappear down the side path, and then, after shaking his fist once more at the gang, he gave a grunt of satisfaction and lumbered back up his garden path.

11

The Key

Jo didn't say a word to Paul about the fight in the street. He knew that if he did, Paul would only use the whole thing as an excuse to tell their mother about the cubs, and Jo was obstinately determined to keep his secret. Anyway, Jo thought, as he had won, Michael Skinner would probably leave them in peace now. He had saved the meat, and for the moment that was what mattered most of all.

A shadow of apprehension lingered in his mind, but he suppressed it, tried to forget about his bruises and made up his mind to enjoy every moment of the cubs. If Paul had known about the fight he would have realized that Michael Skinner wouldn't be content to leave things as they were, and matters might have turned out quite differently in the end. But Paul did not know.

For the next three days everything went well for Paul and Jo. The cubs, who had been in a very weak state when the boys found them, quickly recovered their natural bounce and vigour and seemed to thrive on the diet which Jo had worked out for them. They ate everything which they were meant to eat, and some things that they were not. It seemed that they wanted to chew things all the time, and they spent a great deal of energy each day tearing up the newspaper which the boys used for their bedding and distributing it around the shed in little piles. But Paul and Jo didn't mind clearing up the mess, for the cubs were proving to be so entertaining and affectionate that the boys would have done anything for them, and wanted to be nowhere but in the shed watching them at play and looking after them.

The next day came and went, and the next. The shops were full of chocolate Easter eggs, the breeze blew light and springlike, the sun shone and the thrush sang on the apple tree in the garden of 35 Brownlow Street. Inside the shed the cubs lifted their heads and listened to it, ears pricked in curiosity.

It was not until the third day when Paul and Jo were counting their money that they came up against their first snag.

'Well, that's that,' said Jo, looking up from the tower of pennies which he had built on the floor of the shed. 'Now we'll have to tell Mum.'

'Perhaps we'll be given some money for Easter,' Paul suggested, but Jo shook his head.

'There's not enough to buy meat for even one more day,' he said. 'They'll have to have bread and milk for supper as it is.'

'Perhaps it's just as well,' Paul said. 'This shed's beginning to smell awful.'

Jo nodded in agreement. The foxes did have a strong, musty smell and even with the window open all day it was becoming worse. 'Anyway,' Jo said, 'they need more room to run about now. It's cruel to keep them shut up in here all the time.'

Paul pulled the cub with the white tail towards him and began to stroke its fur. He had always preferred this one and he thought of it now as his own. Because of its tail, which looked as though someone had stuck a blob of cotton wool on the end, he called it Cottontail, and Jo had christened the second and smaller of the two

Kipper. He said that to begin with it was so bony it was like a Kipper. But both cubs were plump now, and it was hard to believe that they were the same pathetic little animals who had waited so patiently on that hillside for the vixen who would never return. Jo and Paul were the ones who brought them food now, and in return they gave the boys all their trust and love.

'Tell you what,' said Paul. 'It can be our Easter present for Mum and Dad. Good Friday is the beginning of Easter isn't it?'

'I think so,' said Jo.

'Well then at breakfast time, we'll just go and fetch them and bring them in, and then we'll tell Mum and Dad all about them. How we found them ...'

'And that we've had them almost a week. We can say they're easy to feed and keep too.' Jo's voice tailed off. It sounded all right the way they said it now, but he wondered whether it would really be like that tomorrow morning.

'Do you think they'll let us keep them?' Paul asked after a pause.

Jo grabbed Kipper and hugged the cub closely against his chest. 'I don't know,' he muttered. 'But anyway we did save their lives and I suppose that's something.' Jo didn't want to think beyond the next day when they would tell their parents about the cubs, because at the back of his mind was the thought that cubs grow up and become large and strong, and even if their mother and father allowed them to keep Cotton and Kipper for a while, it might be cruel to keep them for ever, as though they were animals in a zoo. He decided not to think about parting with the cubs for the present; it was, in fact, difficult to think about anything just then, for Kipper was chewing the sleeve of his jersey.

'Stop that,' said Jo. The cub looked at him and then wriggled free and ran over to the empty dish, looking for food. 'Look,' Jo said to Paul. 'They're hungry again.'

That afternoon Paul and Jo spent some time clearing up the shed. They wanted it to be really clean and tidy for their parents to see the next morning. The cubs watched inquisitively from inside the orange-box where Jo had put them, but before long they became bored and restless, tipped the orange-box over and began chasing one another round the shed until they were put back in the box again by Paul.

The boys spread the floor with layers of fresh newspaper and remade the cubs' nest, and by the time they had finished the shed looked tidier than it had done for days, and it even seemed to smell fresher too.

'But I daresay they'll have made a terrible mess of it by tomorrow morning,' Jo said.

'If only they wouldn't tear up the newspaper,' Paul agreed.

Jo locked the door behind them and put the key in his pocket. Apart from going down there to give the cubs their evening meal they had decided to keep away from the shed for the rest of the day, so as to be sure of keeping the secret until the next morning.

Everything had worked out very well, Paul thought, as he followed Jo into the house. It hadn't been as difficult keeping the secret as he had thought, but he was glad that they were going to tell their parents the next day. The only thing that worried Paul was the disappearance of the gang. Although he didn't know about Jo's fight, he thought it strange that there had been no sign of any of them – even Neville had vanished. The feeling in his bones that all was not well would not leave

95

him. But as he knew that there was no point in saying anything to Jo, he just kept quiet and hoped for the best. Altogether, Paul thought as he closed the back door, it would be a relief when the next day came.

Paul was right to be apprehensive. Five gardens away Neville had just watched him and Jo go back into the house. From his perch in the apple tree he saw them lock the door of the shed, as he had seen them do for the last three days, and he had watched as Jo put the key back in his pocket. He waited until they had disappeared inside the house, and then he scrambled down from his lookout and went to find Michael Skinner.

Neville was too much of a coward to be any good at fighting, and he knew it. But he was good at working things out. After watching Paul and Jo and the shed for the past three days he had formed a plan and the time had come to tell Michael about it. It would have to be tonight, too, Neville thought as he went stealthily towards his front door. His mother was going out to a church meeting, and apart from the lodgers he would have the house to himself.

'Where are you going?' his mother called. 'It's nearly dinner time dear.'

'Back in ten minutes,' Neville lied, and went out banging the front door behind him. It would take him more than ten minutes to get to the playground and back and his mother would be angry with him if he was late for dinner. But Neville didn't care. Michael would be pleased with his plan, he thought, and that was what really mattered.

It was not until after dark that evening that Jo slipped out of the back door and down the garden path. He had two slices of bread and a cup of milk with him for

96

the cubs' supper. Paul had agreed to stay in the house to answer questions in case Jo should be missed. It was later than it should have been for the cubs' meal, but Jo hadn't been able to escape until then. The garden was full of shadows and dark shapes, but Jo's mind was on the cubs and how hungry they must be.

He let himself into the shed and left the key in the padlock and the padlock swinging on the hook as he always did. Inside the shed it seemed darker still and he could hardly make out the cubs. But they had heard him coming and trotted forward to welcome him.

'All right, all right,' Jo muttered, fumbling along the shelf for the dish. It was difficult to see what he was doing at first, but after a while his eyes became accustomed to the gloom and he crumbled the bread into the dish and tipped the milk over it. The cubs were ravenous as usual; Jo sat down to wait, knowing that it wouldn't be long before they finished.

The wind had risen and the garden outside was full of strange tappings and creakings as the branches of the old apple tree swayed and knocked against one another. Once Jo thought that he heard quick footsteps and he strained to listen, but the sound faded immediately and only the window of the shed banged once or twice.

When the cubs had finished their supper Jo still stayed with them. He was reluctant to leave, knowing that the next day everything would be different. Even in the dark he could make out Cottontail by the white tip, but as usual he paid slightly more attention to Kipper. Kipper belonged to him.

'But you're not bony any more,' he murmured as he stroked the cub's fur. Kipper was more affectionate than Cottontail; Jo thought so anyway as he felt the cub's cold sharp nose under his chin and the little body pressed close against him.

'You love me, don't you, Kipper?' he murmured. 'I won't let them take you away from me if I can help it.'

At last, fearful in case his mother should wonder where he was, Jo put the cubs back in their bed, fastened the window securely and went out.

He was only just in time, for at that moment an oblong of light appeared in the side of the house, and he saw his mother standing framed in the kitchen doorway.

'Jo!' she called. 'Jo, where are you?'

'Just coming,' Jo called.

'What on earth are you doing?' his mother asked. 'It's dark.'

'I had to put something away,' Jo answered.

'Well, come on then,' she called. All this time Jo had been feeling for the padlock and the awful realization was beginning to dawn on him that it had gone. It should have been there, on the hook, where he always left it, but it wasn't there. He went down on his hands and knees and began to search around frantically on the muddy ground.

'Come on, Jo,' his mother called again.

Jo knew that he couldn't leave the shed open like that; the cubs would push the door ajar and escape. On the other hand if he told his mother what had happened then the surprise would be spoilt. He stood up again and began to rummage around in his pockets, thinking that perhaps he had put the padlock in one of them by mistake. But it wasn't there. He must have slipped the padlock only a little way through the hook, Jo thought, and a gust of wind had shaken it off. It would be easy enough to find in the morning, but in the meantime he

98

decided to fasten the door with a piece of string which he always carried in his pocket.

'Shan't be a moment,' he called again, and looped the string through the hook and round the catch, tying it as securely as he could. When he was satisfied that nothing could loosen the knots he ran up the path.

'I was just coming to look for you,' his mother said. 'What have you been up to?'

'Nothing much,' said Jo evasively, his mind on the padlock. He still couldn't think where it had gone, or how it had slipped off the hook, and he was also uneasy about the shed, even though he knew the knots were safe.

He didn't say anything to Paul. He would only fuss; and although he wouldn't have admitted it to anybody, by now even Jo was beginning to think that the secret had gone on for long enough.

12

Thief in the Night

Later on that evening the wind dropped and the rain began to fall. Turning over in the night, half asleep and half awake, Paul heard it pattering against the window pane, and the next time he woke he thought he could hear it still. But when he opened his eyes there were patches of sunlight on the wall. He rubbed his eyes, puzzled by the noise he was sure he had heard. There it was again, as though someone were throwing handfuls of something at the window. Then he saw that Jo's bed was empty and immediately he knew what the noise was.

Through the window he could see Jo just stooping to gather up another handful of gravel. Paul grinned. But when he caught sight of Jo's face as he straightened up he knew at once that something was wrong. Jo's expression was heavy, troubled, almost desperate and Paul knocked urgently on the glass to tell him that he would go down as quickly as he could.

Whatever was wrong, Paul realized, Jo must want it kept quiet, or he would have come through the house to wake him. There was a sinking feeling in the pit of his stomach as he finished dressing and pulled on his plimsolls. Without bothering to do them up he slipped out of the room and down the stairs.

The kitchen clock showed a quarter to eight, he noticed, as he passed it. It was only because it was not a working day that his parents were still in bed.

Outside Jo was waiting for him.

'What's up?' Paul asked.

'You'd better come and see,' said Jo grimly, and led the way down the path.

The shed door was open and before Paul had a chance to ask Jo why, he caught sight of the inside of the shed.

For a moment or two Paul was speechless. The shed, their shed which they had left so neat and tidy the night before looked as though it had been hit by an earthquake. The clean newspaper which they had laid on the floor was now torn and muddied with the prints of innumerable shoes. The shelves had all been pulled down and were either swinging by one nail or else lying on the floor. And all their possessions were scattered among the chaos. The cubs' dinner plate was broken, lying in pieces beside the orange-box table which was splintered into fragments on the floor. To add to the confusion everything was soaking wet, for the rain had blown in at the open door throughout the night.

It was a moment or two before Paul caught sight of a

small, huddled shape in the corner, beside what had been the cubs' bed.

'Cottontail,' he whispered. The cub's ears flicked once, but it didn't move. Paul went towards the corner, but Jo held him back.

'You can't get any nearer than that,' he said. 'I've tried.' Paul shook himself free and bent down towards the cub, stretching out his hand. Cottontail gave a vicious snarl and backed farther into the corner. 'I told you,' said Jo. Paul stared at the cub for a moment in disbelief and then turned to Jo.

'Where's Kipper?' he asked.

'That's just it,' said Jo in a flat voice. 'He's gone.'

'Gone?'

'Yes. Disappeared. I've searched and searched, and I've called, but it's no good.'

'But how? I mean – who—?' Paul stopped and stared around him at the ruin and desolation and he felt the tears begin to prick his eyes. 'I just don't understand,' he said angrily. 'You didn't leave the door open last night, did you?' Jo didn't answer, and Paul turned round and saw that he was beginning to colour. 'You couldn't have done,' he said disbelievingly, staring at Jo. 'Well, did you? Did you?'

'Sort of,' Jo muttered. He stuck his hands in his pockets and backed away from Paul a few paces.

'What do you mean – sort of?' Paul shouted.

'Well, if you'd only stop yelling and listen I'd explain,' Jo said wearily. 'I know I should have told you last night, but I didn't think it was important.'

'What wasn't important?'

'When I was feeding them Mum came out and called me,' Jo said slowly and he began to explain to Paul what had happened.

102

'But the padlock couldn't have blown off the hook,' Paul said when Jo had stopped talking.

'I see that now,' Jo nodded miserably. 'But I had to go in, or the surprise would have been ruined. I tied the door up with string. They were good knots, Paul. Honestly. It was quite safe.'

'Huh! Very safe!'

'Well, how was I to know that the padlock had been stolen.'

'Stolen?'

'Well, look,' said Jo waving his arm furiously, 'you don't think I've done all this, do you? Obviously some-one stole the padlock while I was in the shed and then came back again after I'd gone. And did all this. And stole Kipper.' Paul stared at him.

'But who?'

Jo gave a snort. 'I should think you'd be the first per-son to guess that,' he said. 'Michael Skinner and his rotten gang of course. Who else?'

'But Jo, how did they get into the garden?'

'I don't know that,' said Jo. 'But I know it was them,' and he pointed to the corner of the shed. On the wall were the initials M.S. scrawled in red chalk.

Paul sat down heavily on one of the stools and Jo began to kick the door frame with his foot. For a while neither of them spoke and the cub, temporarily for-gotten, crouched in the corner looking from one to the other but not moving.

It was just like the kite all over again, Paul thought. Except that this time it was worse. Far, far worse. And why had the gang done it? Why? And how? And, worst of all, so awful that Paul hardly dared to think about it, only he had to, where was Kipper?

The silence was broken at last by Jo's muffled sobs.

Paul watched him, wishing that he wouldn't cry, but not saying anything, and Jo went on crying and kicking the door frame. Then, inside Paul, something began to happen. Instead of feeling miserable and sorry for himself as he had been doing, he began to feel angry and the anger grew, slowly at first and quietly, but it grew. He had been angry when he had seen the shed, so angry that he had wanted to throw things; but this was different. This anger was cold and thoughtful. Paul found that he could think again now. He stood up.

'Stop crying, Jo,' he said firmly. 'We've got to decide what to do. Have you looked for Kipper in the garden?'

'I told you,' Jo gulped, rubbing his sleeve across his eyes. 'For hours before you were up.'

'And you're sure there isn't a hole anywhere that he could have gone through?'

'I went all round the edge of the garden to make sure,' said Jo.

'Then obviously Michael Skinner's got him,' Paul said calmly.

'We'll never see Kipper again,' Jo wailed, fresh tears pouring down his cheeks. Paul went over and shook him by the shoulders.

'Yes,' he said with icy determination. 'We will.'

'You said that about the kite,' Jo sobbed.

'I know,' said Paul. 'But this time it'll be different. This time they won't get away with it. I promise.' And as he said it he knew that he was right. This time Michael Skinner wasn't going to win because he, Paul, was going to see to it that he didn't. All along he had been afraid that something like this would happen. Now it had happened and he was ready. He wasn't sure yet how he was going to do it, but somehow he was going to get Kipper back and settle with Michael Skinner once and for all.

'Jo,' he said fiercely. 'Stop crying. There's a lot to do.'

'What?' Jo gulped.

'Well, Cottontail for a start. You're the one who's good with animals, remember?' Jo turned and looked where Paul was pointing at the pathetic, wide-eyed little creature in the corner. He brushed the tears from his eyes and nodded.

'OK,' he said.

'And you'll have to tell Mum and Dad something – I don't know what.'

'What are you going to do?'

'I'm going to find Kipper – and Michael Skinner,' Paul said grimly.

'But...'

'Look, this was planned,' Paul interrupted. He looked away from Jo's tear-stained face and out of the shed door down the line of gardens. 'See!' He grabbed Jo's shoulder and swung him round. 'That tree along there. I bet you anything that's in Neville's garden. We know that he was spying on us when we were on the Heath. I bet he's been watching us all the time from up there. Yes...' Paul was working it out as he spoke. 'That's it. It was he who came over and pinched the padlock. Then they all came back together later, the whole gang. They couldn't have come through the back gate because it's locked, and it's too high to climb. They must have come that way.'

'What are you going to do?' Jo asked.

'I'm not sure yet.' Paul narrowed his eyes thoughtfully. 'But I think I know where to begin.'

'Don't you think I'd better come with you?' Jo asked anxiously.

'No.' Paul shook his head. 'I'll be better alone.' He straightened his shoulders and turned to go.

'Here,' said Jo, fumbling in his pocket and pulling out three biscuits. 'You'd better have these.'

'Thanks,' said Paul, smiling grimly. 'Provisions.'

At first as he walked down the street Paul hadn't the least idea what he was going to do, although he had told Jo that he had. The cold, slow anger was still there inside him, though, and his mind was clear. As he walked he thought carefully over what he and Jo knew. The gang had stolen the cub yesterday evening. They had climbed over several garden walls, gone into the shed, wrecked it and taken one of the cubs. Why not both, Paul wondered. It had been dark of course. Perhaps Cottontail had hidden, or run out into the garden and then returned after they had gone. Where, then, had they taken Kipper? Almost at once the answer popped into Paul's head. Michael Skinner was the leader of the gang and the leader always took the booty, so he would have Kipper with him. So far so good. But then Paul came to a full stop because he realized that he didn't know where Michael lived. He was still puzzling over this when he reached the end of the street.

Still deep in thought he turned up the hill, making for the railway bridge. The Heath seemed the obvious place to begin his search. Probably they would have arranged to meet there, either in the playground, or in the hide-out where the kite had fallen that first day. Then Paul remembered that the playground didn't open until nine-thirty. It would still be locked up. That meant that the hide-out would be the most likely place to find them and he would have to hope that he arrived first, or he would be walking straight into a trap.

It all seemed rather a long shot, Paul thought, as he

approached the railway bridge. There might be other places where the gang met, places that he and Jo knew nothing about. He might not see them even though he searched all day. In this vast maze of streets they could be anywhere, just anywhere. And even if he found the gang, that wouldn't necessarily mean that he would find Kipper.

Paul knew all this, yet with dogged determination he went on across the bridge. Something inside him told him that the moment had come. It was he who must find Kipper.

13

The Chase

When Mrs Tomlinson came downstairs to put the kettle on, the first thing she saw was Jo, sitting beside the kitchen table, looking very woebegone, his usually cheerful face streaked with tears and dirt. In his arms was Cottontail.

'Great heavens above, Jo!' Mrs Tomlinson exclaimed. 'What on earth have you got there?' Jo looked up at his mother, and somehow the sight of her standing there in her old blue dressing-gown gave him such a feeling of relief after all that had happened that his eyes brimmed with tears and he began to cry all over again.

'It's Cottontail,' he sobbed, 'it's a fox cub, and we found it. But Kipper's gone, and we don't know where he is and it was meant to be a surprise and now it's all ruined and spoilt, and Kipper's lost . . .' he finished with a sniff. The words had come out in such a muddle and all tripping over one another between the sobs that Mrs Tomlinson didn't really understand anything that Jo had said. But there was one thing she had heard.

'A fox cub?' she asked in astonishment, feeling for a handkerchief and giving it to Jo. Jo nodded. 'Well, you'd better stop crying and tell me how in the world you came to have a fox cub sitting on your knee at nine o'clock on Good Friday morning.' The way his mother said it sounded pretty funny and Jo managed a small smile. 'That's better,' said Mrs Tomlinson. When Jo had blown his nose several times and wiped his eyes he felt better still.

'We never thought you'd believe it,' he said. 'Paul and I couldn't believe it ourselves at first.' He stroked Cottontail's head gently.

Now that Jo had stopped crying Mrs Tomlinson could concentrate better and she pulled out a chair from under the table and sat down in front of Jo, staring hard at Cottontail. The cub gazed back at her without blinking, but his pale eyes were still wide with fear and Jo felt the stiffening of the small body against his chest.

'I think you're right, Jo,' said Mrs Tomlinson at last. 'I do believe it is a cub. But how on earth did you come by it in the middle of London?'

As she spoke she stretched out her hand to stroke the cub, and Cottontail jerked backwards against Jo's chest with a low growl.

'Better not touch,' said Jo quickly. He had had a difficult time catching Cottontail after Paul had gone and he could tell that the cub was still badly frightened. It wouldn't make a very good start if his mother was bitten.

'Where did it come from?' Mrs Tomlinson asked, pulling back her hand.

'We found it – or I should say we found "them",' said Jo.

'Them? However many have you got?' Mrs Tomlinson looked at Jo with a startled expression.

'Only two,' Jo grinned. 'Well, one at the moment because Kipper is lost. Paul's gone to look for him.'

'Two of them,' Mrs Tomlinson said in amazement. Then she put her head on one side and looked hard at Jo. 'I had a feeling that something was going on, but I never dreamed – suppose I make a cup of tea, and then you can tell me all about it.' Jo nodded, and Mrs Tomlinson stood up and ran her hand over his hair. 'You look as though you could do with some tea, and I know I could,' and she went to put the kettle on. When Mr Tomlinson came downstairs to find out why he hadn't had his cup of tea, he found Jo and Mrs Tomlinson still

sitting round the table, with Cottontail sitting up on Jo's knee, drinking tea from a saucer on the table.

So then he had to hear the whole story too, only this time Mrs Tomlinson wanted to tell it, because by now she was bursting with pride over her clever boys. Mr Tomlinson listened, and ran his fingers through his hair. He had only just woken up, and he wondered whether he was still dreaming. When at last Mrs Tomlinson stopped talking for a moment to pour him a cup of tea he asked:

'And where's Paul?'

'He's gone to find Kipper,' said Jo. Mr Tomlinson looked from one to the other of them and then shook his head and took a huge gulp of tea.

'Well I don't know,' he said. 'It all sounds very odd to me. Surely foxes can't live in London, Jo. That doesn't make sense.'

'That's what Paul said when we found the burrow,' Jo grinned. 'And then, when the vixen was killed the cubs were left all alone. They'd have died if we hadn't rescued them, Dad. You will let us keep them won't you? Please. We've looked after them for three days without you knowing. They're no trouble.'

'Three days? Where on earth have you kept them for three days?' Jo explained about the shed and Mr Tomlinson looked at his wife again and drank some more tea.

Jo looked from one to the other anxiously. 'Well?' he asked at last. 'Can we?'

'Well now Jo, we'll have to think about it,' said Mr Tomlinson slowly. 'I'm not making any promises I can't keep. But I must say,' he went on, smiling and looking at Cottontail, 'he's a funny little chap. Good thing you found him. I daresay he wouldn't have had much of a chance on his own.'

'You wait till you see Kipper,' Jo said. 'They're much better when they're together.'

Paul looked out through the thick tangled branches which covered the hide-out. He could see patches of blue sky, and a light wind rattled the twigs together. The floor of the hide-out was still dry, dusty and bare, even after the night's rain and the place smelt dank.

Paul had made himself a peep-hole through which he

111

could see the slope of the hill, the playground and beyond it the bridge. There were few people about, and no one came near the hide-out.

Paul didn't know how long he would have to wait, or what would happen when the waiting was over. He watched a man wheeling his bicycle over the bridge and wondered what he would do if five or six of the gang came all together. Supposing he didn't see them coming and they crept up on him from behind, then he would be trapped. The thought of that made his skin prickle and he looked over his shoulder. But there was no one there.

Part of him thought that it was crazy and pointless to be sitting out there waiting, maybe for nothing, and that part of him wished he was at home having breakfast, or back at Martinford where nightmares like this never seemed to happen. But the other part of him remembered Jo's kite, and Cottontail crouched in the corner of the shed, and the havoc and all the shelves swinging loosely, so he stayed where he was, digging his finger nails into the palms of his hands. Somehow, for Jo's sake and for his own, he had to settle with Michael Skinner once and for all; and somehow he had to get Kipper back. So he knew he must just go on waiting and hoping that one of them would turn up. It wasn't much of a chance and Paul knew it, but it was the best one there was.

As the minutes passed and nothing happened, the waiting became harder and harder for Paul to bear. If he went home now, he began to think, and if he and Jo told their mother and father everything that had happened, then perhaps they would be able to sort things out. This seemed a good idea to Paul until he realized that it wouldn't really solve anything. He and Jo would still have to face Michael Skinner and the gang next term and it was better to settle with him now than to leave it until then. Grown-ups were good at the practical things, like buying clothes, and cooking, and even finding lost socks and marbles, but they couldn't help over something like this.

Suddenly, peering out through the peep-hole, Paul spotted the figure of a boy coming over the bridge. He strained his eyes, pulling the branches farther apart to make the hole larger. The boy turned first towards the playground, and then stopped, and seeming to change his mind, looked up the hill. Paul shrank back. Although well hidden he had the feeling that he might be seen.

The figure began to climb the slope towards him and as he came nearer Paul saw that it was Neville. He was walking hurriedly, looking about him as though he was expecting to see someone. Paul felt his stomach muscles tighten and the blood began to sing in his ears. Neville. What could be better. Neville alone was easy to deal with and he might be persuaded to tell Paul a few facts. Where Michael Skinner lived, for instance. He clenched his fists together and waited.

Neville came almost up to the clump of bushes and then stopped, turned round with his back to Paul and scanned the hillside. For a moment he seemed to be undecided. Then he moved round the clump out of sight.

Paul drew in a deep breath and listened. Let him come in, he thought. Just let him come in. The ambush was perfect. Neville alone and unsuspecting, and Paul waiting, ready for him.

Slowly he turned round and faced the entrance to the hide-out. For a moment there was silence outside, and then he heard footsteps and the sound of the branches being pushed to one side.

Neville came though the entrance on his hands and knees, and Paul pounced on him before his eyes had become accustomed to the gloom and before he had time to straighten up again.

'Got you!' Paul hissed, sitting on his stomach and holding his wrists against the ground.

Thinking it was one of the gang Neville protested mildly. 'Give us a chance,' he mumbled, and then, seeing Paul's face close to his own he gave a gasp of surprise and fright.

'Not much of a fighter, are you?' Paul taunted. Neville wriggled. 'Not so brave when you're on your own, are you?' Paul banged his wrists on to the ground, making him wince.

'You gave me a fright,' Neville whimpered. 'What are you doing here anyway? Better not let the others catch you.' Paul looked down at him in disgust.

'Pity they're not here, isn't it?' he sneered. 'But it doesn't matter because you can tell me where the fox is, can't you?'

'I don't know what you mean,' Neville gasped. 'You're hurting me. I wish you'd get off my stomach.'

'Oh come on,' said Paul. 'The fox cub. The one you and the others stole last night. I want to know where it is.'

Neville stopped wriggling and looked at Paul, his face blank with surprise.

'Did you say fox cub?'

'You must think we're daft,' Paul retorted. 'Michael Skinner even left his initials on the wall. You came over to our place and wrecked the shed, didn't you? And took the fox cub? And you'd better tell me where it is or . . .'

'No!' said Neville. 'Honestly. We didn't take any fox cub.' Paul frowned. It was odd but Neville didn't look as though he was lying. If he was lying he must be a very good actor, Paul thought.

'I'm going to bounce up and down on your stomach until you tell me the truth,' Paul said. 'Like this.' He demonstrated, not very hard, but enough to make Neville let out a howl of fear.

'No, stop,' he whined. 'I'll tell you everything if you get off me.' His eyes were swivelling round and he was trying to look over his shoulder towards the opening. Paul knew he was playing for time, hoping that one of the others would arrive and rescue him. 'Please get off me,' Neville pleaded.

'No,' said Paul. 'But I won't bounce any more if you tell me. And fast.'

'All right,' Neville said, after one more desperate backward glance. 'I'll tell you. We did come. It wasn't my idea,' he lied quickly. 'It was all Michael Skinner . . .'

'Never mind that,' said Paul. 'Go on.'

'But we didn't see any foxes,' Neville stammered. 'There was a puppy, that's all.'

Paul lowered his face towards Neville. 'You're so ignorant you stink,' he said slowly. 'You can't even tell a fox cub from a puppy.'

'I don't believe you,' Neville gasped.

'I don't care whether you believe me or not.'

'And was that what you were carrying – that day when I met you?'

'Yes, and there were two of them. Where's the one you took? That's what I want to know. Where?' He gave another bounce in spite of himself.

'Ow!' Neville howled. 'You said you wouldn't do that any more.'

115

'Well, that one's for wrecking our shed,' said Paul. 'Now where's the cub you stole? Quick, or I'll bounce again.'

Neville swallowed. 'Let me get up,' he said.

'No!'

'When I've told you then?'

'Maybe.'

'Michael took it. There. Now you know everything. Please let me get up. I can't breathe and I feel sick.'

'In a minute,' said Paul, straining his ears for the sound of footsteps outside. It couldn't be long now before one of the others arrived. 'Where does Michael Skinner live?'

'Down there.'

'Address,' said Paul raising himself for another bounce. 'I want his address.'

'Number 8 Goldwell Street, by the tube,' Neville squealed.

'How do I get there?'

'Down the path by the playground to the end of the Heath. It's just there.'

'Sure?'

'I swear it,' Neville spluttered.

'Because if you're wrong you might be sorry ...'

'We didn't mean any harm. Michael always wanted a puppy,' Neville wailed.

'Yah!' Paul hooted and bounced again. 'That's for stealing the kite and for spying on us. And just before I go there is one more thing.' Paul let go of one of Neville's wrists and, quick as lightning whipped off the boy's glasses and tossed them, gently, so as not to break them, towards the other side of the hide-out.

'My specs,' Neville howled. 'If you've broken them I'll ... if they're broken my Mum will kill me ... Oh!'

116

Paul scrambled out into the sunlight again and grinned. 'Too bad,' he muttered, brushing his hands together with satisfaction. 'Too jolly bad.'

He knew he had to hurry. He must get to Michael Skinner's before Michael left to meet the gang and before Neville had time to spread the alarm. Not that Paul thought there'd be much trouble from Neville now. He'd be more likely to go home and lie low after splitting on the rest of the gang like that.

Paul bounded down the hill towards the playground. Neville had been easy to beat but all the same he felt ten feet tall and ready for anything. He wasn't afraid of Michael Skinner any more. He wasn't afraid of anyone.

14

Face to Face

Paul skirted the playground and ran towards the edge of the Heath. The end of the quest seemed to be in sight and after the long wait in the hide-out it was good to be in the fresh air again. He felt good inside too, and if he had had a flag he would probably have waved it in triumph.

But when he reached the end of the Heath and found himself back among the houses again his spirits began to sink. The street Paul was walking down was lined with small, mean-looking houses, brown and dirty. Most of the front doors were open and small children played in the road around their doorsteps. A group of older children were pushing a box on wheels towards the corner. At the end of the street Paul stopped.

He had arrived at Goldwell Street and he had to decide whether to turn right or left. To his right there were only a few houses before the road ended in a brick wall; beyond the wall, he guessed, were the shunting yards and the railway line, and he thought he could hear the sounds of trains. To the left the road ran on until it joined the main road and at the end he could see the round blue and red sign which showed where the tube station was. Paul remembered that Neville had said Michael's house was beside the station and he began to walk towards the sign, counting the numbers on the houses as he went.

His steps became slower and slower and his heart began to pound as he neared the end of the street. For a moment he stopped altogether, his courage ebbing away. Then he thought of Kipper, and Jo at home, waiting for him, and he went on.

Number 20, Number 18, Number 16 . . . Number 10 . . .

As Paul reached the door of Number 8 it opened and Michael Skinner came out. He was carrying a football under one arm and he was alone.

A few yards apart, the two boys faced one another in silence. Without the rest of the gang around him, Paul thought, Michael looked quite skinny and ordinary. He hadn't expected Paul to turn up like this either and it had given him a fright.

Michael was the first to break the silence. He took a couple of steps forward and leant on the gate.

'Come for a game of football then?' he asked, without taking his eyes off Paul.

Paul swallowed and shook his head. 'No. I've come for my fox cub,' he said. 'The one you stole last night.' For a moment a fleeting look of surprise crossed Michael's face. Then he tossed the ball in the air, caught it, and said smoothly:

'You could have joined our game. The others'll be here soon.' The palms of Paul's hands were beginning to feel clammy. He rubbed them on the back of his jeans and took a step forward.

'I want that cub,' he said. 'We know you took it, so you may as well tell me where it is.'

'But I don't know nothing about no fox cub,' Michael said innocently, raising his dark eyebrows and smiling at Paul.

'I've seen Neville,' Paul said. 'I know.' He spoke with meaning, looking straight at Michael. 'Anyway you left

119

your initials on the wall, so we knew it was you. Didn't you think we'd come after you?' Paul had planted himself firmly in front of the gate so that Michael would have to push past him to get out, and Paul could see that behind the casual front which he was trying to keep up, Michael was scared. Down inside him the feeling grew that Michael was a coward; perhaps that was why he needed the gang, to bolster him up. Paul began to feel much braver. 'Look,' he said, 'just tell me where the cub is. I only want it back, that's all.'

Michael studied him for a moment. Then he smiled again and looked beyond him down the street.

'Look,' he said, jerking his head. 'Here are the others now.'

Once the rest of the gang turned up Paul knew that he hadn't a chance. Instinctively he took his eyes off Michael and looked round.

Then everything happened very quickly. He was aware of Michael raising his arm, and he ducked to avoid the blow he thought was coming. As he did so he heard, from his right and behind him, the crash of something falling and breaking. When he turned to see what it was Michael vaulted over the wall and ran off down the street laughing. On the other side of the road where the noise had come from, an old woman was standing with her mouth wide open, staring at the pool of milk and the broken glass at her feet, and the football lay in the middle of the road.

After a moment's silence the old woman began to yell, and simultaneously doors and windows were flung open. Paul didn't wait any longer. He turned and ran down the street in pursuit of Michael, grinding his teeth with fury because he had been tricked.

On the corner he stopped. Michael had disappeared.

120

If he had made for the Heath Paul knew he might as well give up, for he'd never catch him out there. The kids were still playing around with their box cart on the corner.

'That boy,' Paul gasped. 'Which way did he go?' Three of them looked at him blankly. 'Please,' said Paul urgently. 'You must have seen ...'

'I did,' said a little girl. 'There ...' She pointed down the mews.

'Thanks,' said Paul and rushed on.

At the end of Goldwell Street, Paul found that the street turned and ran along beside the railway line. On the railway side there was only the high brick wall, but on the other side were houses. Iron ladders climbed to the upper storeys, but below there were large double doors, and parked outside the doors, all the way down the mews, there were cars in various stages of repair. All the garage doors were closed today, for no one was working and there wasn't a soul about.

If Michael Skinner was down there, then he could only get out the way he had come because the mews was a cul-de-sac. That meant that he would have to come past Paul. 'And this time,' he thought, 'he won't escape so easily.'

Paul wedged himself between one of the cars and the line of garage doors. From there he could look down to the end of the mews, and a large dustbin outside the door gave him partial cover. For a while there was silence and Paul was beginning to wonder whether he had calculated wrongly and if Michael knew of a way out through one of the garages, when he thought he heard footsteps. He peered round the dustbin cautiously, and there, sure enough, a few yards away he could see Michael's feet moving stealthily towards him. 'Got you,'

Paul thought grimly. He smiled to himself and dodged back behind the dustbin, but this time he moved too quickly, nudging the dustbin by mistake with his elbow. With a fearful clatter the lid fell to the ground, clanging on the cobble-stones. Paul bit his lip and groaned inwardly. Michael still had to get past him, but now that he knew he was there the element of surprise had gone.

There was silence while Paul waited to see what would happen.

Suddenly the silence was broken by furious barking. Paul jerked his head up and listened. The barking went on and on, rising to a crescendo and broken up with growls and snapping noises.

It was close too. For one panic-stricken moment Paul thought that the dog was coming for him. He stood up and looked around, but he could see nothing. There was no sign of the dog, and no sign of Michael either. The barking continued though, on and on, and in the midst of it, suddenly, a single yell which made Paul prickle all over with fear.

He darted into the middle of the street and looked around. Why didn't someone come? The place was deserted. There was only the barking.

The sound of the cry still seemed to ring in Paul's ears. He felt sure that Michael was in real danger, yet he hesitated. He had been tricked once already. What if this was a trap too? But the cry had sounded real enough. Horribly real. He began to move doubtfully towards the noise.

He found the place easily enough. One of the double doors was slightly ajar and from inside the garage the noise came clearly to meet him. As he approached he could hear other sounds as well. There was the rattle of a chain, and in the background a low moaning.

At first when Paul peered round the door he could see little, for it was dark inside. Then he made out the dog. It was tethered by a chain to the wall on the left of the garage, but it had pulled the chain as far as it would go and was straining at it, still barking furiously at a huddled-up shape at the back of the garage.

At first the dog didn't see him, so intent was it on its prey, and Paul had a moment in which to watch and think. He saw at once what must have happened. Michael had slipped inside the garage, intending to hide until Paul went away, and the dog had attacked him. Now he was trapped in the corner. He was just out of the dog's reach, but he couldn't get past it again and there was no other way out.

The dog was an Alsatian, the most evil and ferocious-looking beast that Paul had ever seen. It had stopped barking at last, but lay crouched to spring, its ears laid flat on its head and hackles raised, showing a number of teeth as it snarled viciously from time to time.

When Michael at last looked up and saw Paul standing by the door he moaned more loudly than ever.

'Can't you do something?' he stammered.

The dog, who until then had not been aware of Paul's presence, turned its head and gave him a look which made him shrink with fear. It was only with an effort that he stood his ground and looked the dog in the face. For a few moments he was tempted to run away. There was, after all, no reason why he should stay and help Michael. There were plenty of reasons why he should turn his back and walk away from him. Except that Paul knew it could have been him in that corner.

'I'll go and find someone to help,' Paul muttered.

'No! No!' Michael shrieked, suddenly more terrified than ever. 'Don't leave me. Please don't go. Suppose the chain breaks. Please . . .'

'Can't you make a dash for it,' Paul suggested. But even as he said it he saw that it would be no good. Michael was shaking so much that he didn't look as though he could walk, let alone run, and anyway the dog would be sure to catch him before he reached the door.

'My leg,' he moaned, shaking his head, 'he's bitten my leg.'

Paul clenched his fists and edged round the door. It's only a dog, he thought, just a dog.

Trying to keep his voice calm and to feel unafraid he said softly, 'Good boy. Here, good dog.'

The dog turned to him with a furious snarl which showed all its teeth, and tensed, ready to spring. Paul backed hastily away again and leant against the door. He could hear Michael's teeth chattering with fear.

'Don't worry,' he said. 'I'll think of something. You all right?'

'My leg,' Michael murmured. 'There's blood all over the floor.' Paul put his hand in his pocket to get out a handkerchief and as he did so he felt something.

The biscuit. The last biscuit of the three which Jo had given him. He had eaten the other two while he waited for Neville. He took it out and looked at it. It was a bit crumbly round the edges, but that didn't matter. The trick had worked with the fox cubs. Perhaps it would work with the dog. It had to work.

He broke off a small piece of the biscuit and, trying to keep his voice friendly, he moved closer to the dog again.

124

'Good dog,' he said. The dog took its eyes off Michael and regarded Paul suspiciously, but without growling. Paul held out the biscuit so that the dog could smell it, but not reach it, and then tossed it to the ground just in front of the animal. After a moment's inspection it ate it, but as soon as Paul took a step forward again it growled menacingly.

Obviously this wasn't the kind of dog you could make friends with. Probably it was a guard dog that had been trained to attack intruders. Paul put the remains of the biscuit back in his pocket.

Michael was crouching in the right-hand corner, by the back wall. Paul thought that if he could throw the biscuit towards the back left-hand corner, in three bits one after the other, then it might distract the dog for long enough to allow Michael to get out of the garage before it had finished eating.

'Can't you do something,' Michael moaned.

'Yes,' said Paul. 'But you have to help. Are you ready to make a dash for it?'

'No. I can't!'

'It'll be all right,' said Paul. 'Look, I've got some biscuit here and I'm going to throw it – over there.' He pointed. 'When I say run, then you must run, and while the dog's looking for the biscuit you can get out.'

'But I can't run – my leg—'

'You'll have to try,' said Paul impatiently. 'It's not far, and it's the only hope. Or else I can go and get help.'

'No, don't go. Please don't go.'

'Will you try then?' Michael shivered, and the dog looked at him and gave a low growl.

'I can't,' Michael wailed, looking at it.

'Oh well,' said Paul angrily. 'If you're too scared even

125

to try, I'm going. You can find someone else to get you out.'

'No!' Michael shrieked in real terror. 'Don't go. I'll do anything you say. Anything. Only please don't go.'

'OK, OK,' said Paul. 'It'll be all right. Really.'

'Sure?'

'Sure,' said Paul, crossing his fingers behind his back. It had to be. It was the only thing he could think of. 'Get ready now,' he said.

He pulled the biscuit out of his pocket again and broke it into three pieces. With an effort Michael raised himself to a sprinting position and as he did so the dog began to snarl again. Paul knew that with every moment that passed Michael would become more frightened. There was not a second to lose.

'Ready?' he asked.

Michael nodded.

'Don't forget, when I say "Go".' He held the biscuit out towards the dog again and when he was sure that he had smelt it, he threw the first piece. The dog went after it, searching along the ground. Quickly Paul threw the other two pieces, and as he did so he shouted.

'Go! Now! QUICK.'

For a sickening moment Michael didn't move. The dog was gobbling the biscuit up as hard as it could; another second and it would be finished ...

'RUN!' Paul yelled. With a sudden effort Michael threw himself towards the door and Paul was just in time to grab him by the shoulder and pull him outside before the dog rounded on them both, barking with renewed fury and arching itself to spring.

Paul pushed the door shut with his shoulder and leant against it, looking at Michael. He was as white as chalk except for his eyes which seemed darker than ever

against the pallor of his face. Paul saw that he was still shaking and he looked near to tears. On the other side of the door the dog continued to bark.

'Let's get out of here,' Paul said. 'Can you walk?' He looked down at Michael's leg. His trousers were torn and the blue material was stained and soaked with blood. He nodded and began to hobble up the street beside Paul. 'Think you'd better go to the hospital or anything?' Paul asked.

' 'Orrible brute,' Michael muttered. 'I'd cut its throat if I could. They didn't ought to leave a dangerous dog like that unguarded. I might have been killed.'

'It's not really the dog's fault,' Paul said reasonably. 'That's what it's there for – to stop people trespassing.' The last ten minutes had driven all thought of Kipper out of his head, but now he remembered again. 'Anyway,' he said, 'I reckon you owe me something now. So where's my fox cub?'

Michael looked at him briefly and shook his head. Paul caught him by the arm.

'Look,' he shouted, 'if it wasn't for me you'd still be in there with that dog. It was me that rescued you and you know it. Now tell me what you've done with the cub.'

'Let go,' Michael muttered. 'My leg's hurting.'

'You tell me first,' said Paul fiercely. His eyes were blazing and he had gone very pale himself.

'I don't know where it is,' Michael muttered, his eyes down.

'Yes you do,' Paul said scornfully. He shook Michael's shoulder and the boy winced with pain.

'Look,' he said with an effort. 'I didn't know it was a fox cub. That's the truth. I thought it was a puppy.'

'I know all that,' said Paul. 'Where is it, though?

That's all I want to know. Where is it?'

Michael looked at Paul and his dark eyes were defiant in spite of everything that had happened.

'All right,' he said. 'I'll tell you. I got as far as the Heath with it, and then it escaped. So now you know. Your fox cub's run away.'

15

The Search

Paul let go of Michael's shoulder and stared at him. Just for a moment he wondered whether to believe him; but there was really no doubt about it. Michael was telling the truth.

'You fool,' Paul said. 'You stupid ignorant – you fool. All you can do is wreck things. You can't even look after yourself without your stupid gang around you, and when people try to do ordinary things and have fun, like flying kites, all you can do is try to spoil everything. I wish I hadn't rescued you from that dog. I wish I'd left you in there and gone away and not told anyone. I could have done ... that's what you and your gang would have done isn't it? I wish I'd never seen you. And I never want to see you again. Well, from now on you'd just better leave us alone, or it will be the worse for you. Understand? Just leave us alone.'

Michael had covered his face with his hands. Paul thought he was crying but he didn't care. He shoved his hands deep into his pockets and walked away.

So it had all been for nothing. The fight with Neville, and chasing Michael and rescuing him from the dog – all useless. All – nothing.

And it was wrong, Paul thought passionately. Wrong that it should end like this. He should have found Kipper. Now, right now he should be triumphantly carrying the cub home to Jo. But instead of that Kipper was lost, wandering about somewhere on the Heath, or perhaps dead on the railway line. They'd never see Kipper again. And he had to go home and tell Jo what had happened.

He wasn't a hero after all. He was a failure. Far away across the Heath a church bell began to toll mournfully; the wind had freshened and scudding grey clouds blotted out the sun.

The dreary walk home was the worst thing Paul had ever known; worse even than the first lonely weeks in London, for there was nothing to keep him company as he trudged along but the knowledge that he had failed.

When he reached home Jo was sitting on the front wall waiting for him.

'It wasn't any good, Jo,' Paul said. 'I tried, but it wasn't any good.' He stopped for a moment, unable to say anything else.

'What happened?' Jo asked.

'They've lost Kipper. Somewhere on the Heath,' Paul couldn't look at Jo any longer. He walked past him, brushing the hopeless, angry tears away with the back of his hand and rushed into the house and upstairs.

After a while he heard the bedroom door open and his mother came and leaned over him.

'Paul,' she said gently. 'Paul, whatever is the matter?' Paul hit the pillow with his fist and turned his face to the window.

'I just want to be left alone,' he muttered. 'I don't want to answer a lot of questions, that's all.' His mother, who had caught a glimpse of his white, exhausted face said kindly 'Well suppose I bring you up some cocoa — and some toast. Would you like that?'

After a moment Paul nodded. 'And Cottontail,' he said.

'What's up?' Mr Tomlinson asked when his wife came back into the kitchen.

She shook her head. 'I can't tell yet. But he's very upset. Says he won't answer a lot of questions. Now where's the cub gone. He says he wants Cottontail.'

'I thought he'd gone to look for the other cub.'

'Well, he hasn't found it,' said Mrs Tomlinson. 'You'd better ask Jo what's going on. Paul's quite done in. Ah, there you are you rascal,' she finished up, going down on her hands and knees and peering under the table where Cottontail was contentedly chewing a corner of the rug.

Mr Tomlinson found Jo in the shed, sitting dejectedly on one of the upturned orange-boxes. He stood in the doorway and stared at all the wreckage.

'What's been going on here, Jo?' he asked.

'Nothing much,' Jo muttered.

'Oh yes it has. I can see that it has. Now look here, Jo, it's time that you told me the whole story if you and Paul are going to keep that cub. I want to know what's been happening. Your mother and I have a right to know, and Paul won't answer any questions at present, so it'll have to be you.'

All at once Jo realized what his father had just said.

'Did you say? . . .'

'I said if you're going to keep the cub then I want to know what's been going on,' Mr Tomlinson said firmly, but he smiled at Jo as he said it.

'Do you mean we can keep Cottontail then?'

'He's going to be fully-grown fox one day, Jo, don't forget that. But in the meantime – well I don't see why not. But . . .' Mr Tomlinson held up his hand to stop Jo from interrupting, 'you've got to tell me about all this . . .' he waved his hand round the shed. 'And where's Paul been to this morning?'

132

In the end Jo told his father almost everything, but not quite. He still didn't want to say anything about the gang until Paul was there. But by the time Jo had finished talking Mr Tomlinson had a pretty good idea about the bits he hadn't mentioned, as well as everything that he had, and he decided that for the time being he would let sleeping dogs lie. Jo was upset by the disappearance of the cub, and since it seemed unlikely that it would ever turn up again Mr Tomlinson didn't want to be too hard on him at the moment.

'We'll have another talk about it later when Paul comes down,' said Mr Tomlinson, putting his arm round Jo's shoulder. 'Why don't you take the football out into the garden now? No sense in brooding is there?'

Later when Paul came downstairs with Cottontail in his arms he went straight out into the garden. He didn't want to talk to his mother or father, but he had to talk to Jo.

They sat on the upturned orange-boxes and Paul told him everything that had happened, carefully leaving out any mention of the dog. He didn't want to talk about that yet.

When he had finished talking there was silence between them for a little while. Then Jo said, 'Perhaps Kipper will find the way back here. Dogs do, don't they? Kipper might, too, don't you think?'

'Maybe,' said Paul doubtfully. He didn't think there was any hope really.

'They might have looked for him – when he escaped last night, I mean. Why didn't they look?'

Paul shrugged, holding Cottontail closely. 'It must have been dark I suppose. I don't know ...' the words kept petering out between them. 'Well, at least we've still got Cottontail, and he can belong to both of us now.'

'Do you suppose,' said Jo, 'that if we went and looked for Kipper ... I mean it might be worth trying, mightn't it?' His voice trailed away. In the distance they heard a front-door bell ring.

Cottontail nudged Paul under the chin and struggled to get down. All the scents and sounds of the garden were wafting in through the shed door and having recovered from his experience of the night before the cub was eager to be out exploring. As soon as Paul put him down he frisked through the door and across the grass, tail lashing in delight.

It was then that Mrs Tomlinson called to them from the back door. 'Paul – Jo – there's a visitor to see you.'

Standing beside their mother was Michael Skinner. Paul could see that his leg was swathed in large quantities of bandage, and as he came towards the shed he looked uneasy, almost shy. Cottontail had stopped playing and stood in the middle of the grass watching Michael warily.

Jo saw Michael stretch out his hand to the cub, but Cottontail jumped backwards and gave a low growl.

'No wonder,' said Jo with a snort, and Paul muttered, 'What's he doing here anyway? I told him I never wanted to see him again,' and he turned his back on Michael's approaching figure.

Michael came as far as the door of the shed. Standing there he couldn't avoid seeing the damage that he and the gang had done the night before. He looked quickly down at the ground and Jo realized that he was actually feeling ashamed at what he saw.

'Well? What do you want?' Jo asked him.

'I've – er – I've come to say sorry. About the fox cub and that ... and ...' he waved his hand towards the

134

inside of the shed, 'and all this.' There was a short silence. Michael looked out across the grass, and Jo didn't know what to say. 'And to say thank you to him ...' Michael went on jerking his head towards Paul, '... for the dog ...'

'Dog? What dog?' Jo asked, frowning.

'Come on. You know what dog,' Michael said.

'Honestly I don't,' said Jo, shaking his head.

'You mean he didn't tell you?' Michael was incredulous.

'No, he didn't. You tell me. Go on.'

So Michael told him, and Jo sat listening, looking at Paul and nodding until Michael had finished.

'Wow!' he said then. 'Wow-ee!'

'Oh it was nothing,' Paul mumbled. 'Forget it, can't you.'

There was another embarrassed silence and then Jo said, 'Yes, let's forget it. I'm meant to be the one who's good with animals – not you ...' and he grinned at Paul. Paul smiled back and then they both began to laugh. Michael looked from one to the other of them, and then he smiled too.

'Look,' he said suddenly, 'I thought it was a bit daft, what we did last night. I thought we'd, that is the gang and me, I thought we'd have a search – for the cub. We didn't really mean it to be like this, you see,' he looked at the shed again. 'We didn't mean to keep the cub – just give you a fright. We didn't know it was a cub even. We thought it was a puppy.'

'Well, you gave us a fright all right,' said Jo bitterly.

Michael nodded. 'But we're going to search,' he said earnestly. 'We might find it. You never know. Well, that's all really.' He turned and started to walk away.

'Hey, wait a moment,' Jo called after him. 'Why – I

135

mean why did you do it? The kite and everything? Why us?'

Michael looked embarrassed. 'Dunno really,' he mumbled. Then after a pause in which he furrowed his brow. 'We didn't know you, you see. Anyway, that's what a gang's for, isn't it?'

Paul looked at Jo to try and tell him not to ask any more questions. After all, Michael had said he was sorry. Jo did mutter something about it being cuckoo to go round wrecking things, but he said it so quietly that Michael couldn't hear.

'Tell you what,' said Michael coming back, 'why don't you come too?'

Paul and Jo looked at one another and then Paul said, 'Yes. OK, we'll come.'

At the end of the street the gang were waiting. Even Neville was there. There were eight of them altogether, counting Neville and Michael. They seemed all right now; in fact they seemed quite friendly.

'That's Johnny,' Michael began, reeling off their names, 'and Keith and Andrew (they're twins) and Peter, but we call him Lugger ...'

'Because of his big lug-holes,' the others chorused.

They all nodded their agreement when Michael said that Paul and Jo were going to help search. He was still the leader, but somehow Paul felt that he had changed. Everything seemed to be suddenly different. He looked at Jo standing squarely beside him, and thought that if they could just find Kipper everything would be really good, better than he could have dreamed.

They searched all afternoon. Michael directed them from the top of the hill, and the others fanned out in twos and threes, searching every ditch and hollow,

136

around every tree and even along beside the railway line because Jo said that was the obvious place to look. They found a great number of things – several old shoes, a half-full packet of cigarettes, a dead rat, and old newspapers and lollipop wrappers that would have filled several baskets. But there was no sign of Kipper.

'Tomorrow morning again then,' said Michael when they all assembled once more on the top of the hill. 'You two are coming back, aren't you?'

Paul looked at Jo and nodded. 'You bet,' he said.

'It won't be any good, though,' said Jo sadly as they walked home.

'It might be,' said Paul. 'You never know.' But privately he thought that Jo was right.

By lunch time on Saturday they were all beginning to give up hope. They stood in a group, tousled and dejected with Michael in the centre.

'We'll go on again after lunch,' he said doggedly. More than any of them he wanted the cub to be found, for it was the only thing that could really settle his debt to Paul, and he knew it.

'No,' Paul broke in suddenly. 'Jo and I have decided. We've talked it over and we know it's no good. Either Kipper has run miles away, or else he has been found by someone, so there's no point in going on looking.'

It was Jo's cub though, and they all looked at him for confirmation. Slowly Jo nodded his agreement. A look of relief crept over some of the gang members' faces; it had been hard work searching, and most of them wanted to go to the fair. The tantalizing sound of the merry-go-rounds and the hum of the engines had carried across the Heath towards them all morning.

The group was just beginning to disperse when Neville had his good idea.

'Hang on,' he said slowly, pushing his glasses up his nose with one finger. 'There is one place we haven't tried looking.' They all turned to him.

'Well? Let's have it then,' Michael prompted eagerly.

'If we thought it was a puppy, then someone else might have thought the same thing. I mean not many people know there are foxes in Hampstead, do they?'

'Go on,' said Jo.

'Well, if someone found it and thought it was a puppy – there's only one place where they take stray dogs isn't there . . . ?'

'Of course,' Michael shouted, clicking his fingers. 'Battersea Dogs' Home.'

Neville nodded. 'Worth a try anyway, don't you think?'

'Great idea!' said Michael.

Paul and Jo were puzzled. 'Where is this place?' Paul asked. 'I've never heard of it.'

'Nor me,' said Jo.

'Never heard of Battersea Dogs' Home!' the gang chorused.

Jo flushed. 'We don't know much about London,' he said hotly, 'but at least we can tell the difference between a fox and a dog.'

Paul intervened. 'All right, Jo,' he said laying a hand on his arm, and then turning to Michael and Neville. 'If you think that Kipper might be there, let's go and see.'

Michael nodded. 'We can't all go though. It's on the other side of London, you see, and we'll have to go by bus.' He looked round at them all.

'Me,' said Neville. 'It was my idea.'

'Right,' said Michael. 'And Paul and Jo. And me. Just the four of us. OK, everyone? And we'll meet on the corner of Brownlow Street at two o'clock. You others can go to the fair.'

Perhaps it was because the sun came out as they walked home, but Jo's hopes suddenly began to rise.

16

The Last Chance

When Mr Tomlinson had heard about the plan at lunch he had said it was the most hare-brained scheme he had ever come across, and there wasn't the slightest chance of finding Kipper. How did they propose to get to Battersea, which was miles away, he wanted to know. Paul said that all lost or stray dogs were taken to Battersea – Michael had said so. And they could get a bus all the way. In the end Mr Tomlinson reluctantly agreed.

'But if you don't find the cub,' he said sternly, 'then that's that. You can't go on and on looking. It might be anywhere by now. So after today we forget all about it. And after all there's still ... ouch ...' Cottontail interrupted by chewing his shoe-laces under the table and had to be picked up and scolded.

'It's the not knowing that's so awful,' Jo had tried to explain.

'I understand,' his father said, patting his shoulder. 'And I suppose there is a slim chance that you might find the cub this afternoon, but don't build up too much hope, will you?'

'You have to give up sometime, Jo,' said his mother.

'After this afternoon then,' Jo nodded. 'I promise.' He took a deep breath and screwed his eyes tight shut. 'I promise to try and forget all about Kipper after this afternoon,' he said with a rush. When he opened his eyes his mother was smiling at him lovingly.

'Good boy,' his father said, nodding with approval. But it didn't seem much of a promise to Jo because by then he was absolutely certain that they were going to find Kipper at Battersea.

The four of them sat on the top deck during the bus journey, looking out of the window and talking. Paul and Jo learnt a great deal about London from Michael and Neville.

'This is Park Lane – where the nobs stay,' said Michael as they bowled along past the luxury hotels on one side and the park, where all the daffodils were blowing in the breeze on the other side.

'Hyde Park,' said Neville jerking his thumb.

As the bus crossed the river, the gulls wheeled and chattered above the glittering water and an afternoon pleasure steamer plied its slow way upstream; they were almost there. On the other side of the river it was a different London altogether, more homely, with rows and rows of red-brick terraced houses.

'Battersea,' shouted the conductor and they swung down the length of the bus and clattered down the stairs, out onto the pavement.

'Which way?' Paul asked.

Michael looked round. 'Don't know,' he said. 'Do you, Neville?'

Neville shook his head and pointed to a man selling evening papers on the corner. 'He'll know,' he said. The others waited while he went to ask.

'Round the corner and first on the left,' Neville said when he came back. 'He asked if we were going to buy a dog.'

The man at the entrance to the Dogs' Home asked

the same question, 'Because you can't buy a dog unless you have a grown-up with you,' he said, looking disapprovingly at the four of them.

'We don't want to buy one. We're looking for one that's lost,' Michael said.

'Right you are,' and the man waved them in.

Inside there were rows and rows of wire enclosures, like a zoo, and behind every fence there were dogs. Small and large, fat and thin, pedigree and mongrel, black, brown, grey and white, long-haired dogs and short-haired dogs, dogs with pricked ears and dogs with floppy ears, short-tailed and long-tailed and dogs with no tail at all. But whatever their shape, size or colour, all the dogs had one thing in common. They were all lost and they all looked up hopefully as the boys went by.

'Never seen so many dogs in my life,' said Neville.

'Hey, look at this little white one,' said Michael. 'I like him. Here, boy, here. He's only a baby too. Hey you three, look, he's licking me.'

Jo walked on, searching, running his eye over every dog and hardening his heart against the pathetic looks. He was only interested in finding one face and until he found it he would not be happy. He turned once and looked for the others. But they were dawdling, yards away. He went on.

When Jo reached the end of the row, he turned and came back down on the other side. His hopes were beginning to dwindle, but he hadn't given up.

Suddenly he stopped. At the far end of this particular enclosure, there was a brown shape, huddled up, nose to tail, asleep. Jo began to bob about, trying to get a closer look and becoming more and more excited.

'Hi! You lot,' he called to the others. 'Come and see

this.' The other three had gone back to the enclosure with the little white dog in it and were sticking their fingers through the wire and talking to it. But when they heard Jo call they ran over to him.

'Look,' said Jo pointing. 'Look, over there in the corner. Kipper, Kip-kip,' he called, pressing his nose against the wire. The bundle in the corner moved at last, looked around, stood up and stretched, wakened by all the noise, and as it did so Jo's heart sank. He looked at the others and shook his head slowly. He had been so sure. The mongrel came across the enclosure looking enquiringly at the boys. Jo turned away.

'I thought it was,' he muttered to Paul. 'I really did.'

'Cheer up,' said Paul. 'Kipper's much nicer than that mangy mongrel anyway. Have you looked in all the cages yet?'

'No,' said Jo. 'Not yet.' But as he looked down the line he saw that there were only six more enclosures left.

'I'll look with you,' said Paul.

They moved more and more slowly and spent longer and longer beside each enclosure. But at the end they were back where they had started.

'It's no good,' said Jo. 'Kipper's not here after all.' The others looked at him silently.

'We could ask,' said Michael. 'Ask someone ...'

Paul nodded and went up to one of the attendants.

'Excuse me,' he said, 'but is this all?'

'All?' asked the man. 'Isn't it enough?'

Paul shook his head sadly. 'No,' he said. 'Ours isn't here.'

'Are you sure now?'

'Quite sure,' said Paul. 'I don't suppose,' he went on

desperately as the man turned to go, 'that you've seen a – a fox cub have you?'

'Good grief,' said the man, swinging round again. 'Did you say fox cub?' Paul nodded. 'This isn't a zoo, you know. We've got our work cut out looking after dogs, never mind foxes,' and he went off shaking his head and muttering, 'fox cub indeed ... Kids ...'

'No good,' said Paul sadly as he rejoined the others.

Suddenly Jo had had enough. He wanted to get out, away from all those pleading eyes in the enclosures.

'This place gives me the creeps,' he said savagely. 'Come on, let's go.'

'I'm sorry, Jo,' said Paul when they were outside in the road again. Jo had stopped and was looking back at the gate.

'It's all right; I never thought it would be any good anyway,' he lied.

'Kipper might still turn up,' said Michael. 'You never know.'

'That's right,' Neville nodded.

Jo looked at the solemn faces of the other three. He was the youngest of the group but suddenly he felt older than any of them.

'No,' he said. 'You never know. Anyway, there's still Cottontail. Probably it's a good thing. One will be easier to look after than two, and they're a lot of work ...' his voice petered out and he looked down the road.

Paul stared at him in admiration. He knew what it must have cost Jo to say that. He had been so sure of finding Kipper that afternoon.

'Well anyway,' Michael said after a moment or two, 'you two are in the gang now, you and Paul. If you want to be, that is.' He was making amends by offering them the only thing he had to offer and Paul knew it.

'We'd like that, wouldn't we Jo,' he said quickly, and Jo nodded.

On the corner Michael remembered that he had to buy an evening paper for his mother.

'Every Saturday,' he explained, 'so that she can check her pools. One day we'll win twenty thousand, and then we'll be rich. We won't live in Goldwell Street any more. We'll have a whopping great house somewhere, with a swimming-pool in the back garden, and we'll have chicken for lunch every day.'

On the top of the bus they went on talking about winning the pools. They were all trying to cheer up Jo.

'You could go and stay in one of those posh hotels in Park Lane whenever you wanted,' said Neville.

'Yuh,' Michael nodded. 'And we'd have a red sports car too, and drive up and down the motorway at ninety—'

'A hundred,' said Neville.

'A hundred and fifty!' said Paul. Michael used the paper as a steering-wheel and cornered sharply, making a brake-screaming noise as he did so. The others laughed.

'Hey, what does your Dad do?' Paul asked. Michael dropped the paper on the seat beside him and frowned.

'How should I know,' he said sullenly. 'He walked out when I was a kid. I haven't seen him since.'

'Oh,' said Paul awkwardly. He looked at Neville, who shrugged his shoulders. 'I'm sorry,' said Paul after a pause.

'It's OK,' Michael answered. 'Why should I care?' But he went on staring moodily at the floor of the bus.

'Here,' said Neville, suddenly breaking the silence. 'Let's see who won the big match.' He picked up the

145

paper and began skimming through it. Paul and Jo looked over his shoulder.

'It's not here,' said Neville.

'Must be too early,' said Michael.

'And the results aren't here either – that means you've wasted sixpence . . .'

'Hey! Wait a minute,' Jo said suddenly. 'What's that?'

'What?'

'The page before.' He had gone very red and was leaning over the seat. 'Quick,' he said, 'turn back.' Neville flicked the page over again. 'Look,' said Jo. 'Look at that.' He pointed to a photograph at the top of the page. 'It's Kipper – I tell you it's Kipper,' he shouted, trying to grab the paper. Neville jerked it away.

'Hang on a sec,' he said. 'Let's have a look.' With maddening slowness he pushed his glasses up with his finger and peered closely at the photograph, while Michael looked over his shoulder and Paul and Jo craned over the seat. The picture showed a policeman, smiling widely and holding in his arms what looked like a fox cub.

'It is,' said Jo. He was scarlet now and his eyes were blazing.

'Meet the new occupant of cell number 8, Hampstead Police Station,' Neville read. 'This little fellow was found by Constable Price wandering on the Heath early this morning. "He certainly enjoys a good cup of tea," says Constable Price . . . And what is it? A fox cub . . .'

'There you are,' Jo said, jumping up and down in his excitement. 'It says it's a fox cub. It says so, doesn't it?'

'But it doesn't say it's Kipper,' Paul objected.

'But I can see it is,' Jo retorted. 'I'd know Kipper anywhere.'

'You can't be sure till you actually see the cub,' Paul insisted. It all seemed too good to be true and he didn't want Jo to be disappointed again.

'It must be though,' said Michael. 'It was found on the Heath.'

'Where's the Police Station?' Jo asked.

'We know,' said Neville. 'We'll take you there.'

It wasn't very far from the bus stop to the Police Station and the four boys ran most of the way. Neville, who wasn't as fast as the others, arrived a few seconds after them, and was in time to see Jo opening the paper and showing the picture to the Desk Sergeant who was eyeing them all silently from behind the counter.

'We've come about this,' said Jo breathlessly.

'Yes?' said the Sergeant.

'It's his cub,' said Michael.

'Yes, that's right. It's my cub,' Jo nodded. 'It's called Kipper.' The Sergeant was tall and very solid looking. He studied each of the four in turn and then, leaning on the counter he pointed his pencil at Jo.

'You,' he said. 'How do you know it's yours?' Immediately the other three began talking, but Jo was silent. He had realized that the Sergeant wasn't going to hand Kipper over just because Jo said the cub belonged to him. He would have to convince him of the truth of his story first.

'Quiet,' said the Sergeant. 'I want to hear what he's got to say.'

'I think the cub must be mine,' Jo began carefully, 'because I lost him on the Heath on – Thursday night. If I could see him, then I'd know.'

'Mm,' said the Sergeant thoughtfully. 'Can you describe the animal?' Jo frowned.

147

'It's got a white chest,' he said, 'but no white tip to its tail. The other one has, though . . .'

'Other one?'

'The one at home. There were two you see,' Jo explained. 'We found them – the vixen had been killed on the railway line, and so we took the cubs home. They were starving – they would have died. It wasn't stealing, was it?' he asked anxiously. For the first time the Sergeant smiled. Then he turned to the Constable who was sitting behind a typewriter farther back and listening.

'If you can tear yourself away,' he said with mock politeness, 'would you mind fetching that – er—' he cleared his throat, 'that fox cub, Constable.'

'Thanks,' said Jo. 'Thanks so much.'

'Not so fast,' said the Sergeant. 'We haven't finished yet, you know.'

Jo looked round at the others. Michael winked and Paul crossed his fingers in front of him so that Jo could see. Neville was staring curiously at everything in the Police Station and whistling under his breath.

In a moment the Constable came back, carrying a brown, furry object.

'What shall I . . .'

'Over here on the desk,' said the Sergeant, clearing all the papers to one side, and the Constable put the cub down gingerly in front of him. Jo took a step forward.

From that moment on it was clear to all of them that the cub was Kipper and that he knew whom he belonged to. After smelling Jo's outstretched hand and looking at him intently for a moment, the little fox went wild with joy, jumping up and down and scrabbling at Jo's chest until he picked him up off the counter. Then he nestled against Jo and, nudging him under the chin with

his nose, wriggled and squirmed, all the time growling softly with delight.

'Steady on,' said Jo, beaming all over his face. By now everyone was smiling, even the Sergeant, and the other three crowded round all trying to stroke the cub. At last the Sergeant cleared his throat and said, 'that seems to settle the matter – so you lot had better get off home.'

'You mean we can go?' Jo asked.

'That's right, lad.' And then in a firmer voice he added, 'But see you take better care of him from now on. Not everyone has a fox cub as a pet.'

'I know,' said Jo, grinning widely.

Outside the others gathered round him again.

'Bit of luck, wasn't it,' Michael said. 'Suppose I hadn't bought that paper.'

'Or if I hadn't looked at it,' said Neville.

'Yes,' said Paul. 'Everything's turned out fine.'

They walked up the road, making for Brownlow Street.

'You coming back with us?' Paul asked.

Michael shook his head. 'Got to go now,' he said. 'See you tomorrow. I'll come round and help sort the shed out if you like.'

'Then you can see both cubs together,' said Jo happily.

'I'll come too,' said Neville, 'and I'll bring the padlock and key. I've got them at my place.'

'Tomorrow then,' said Michael when they reached the corner of Brownlow Street. 'By the way,' he added, flicking back the lock of dark hair from his forehead, 'I thought we might try and get bikes for the summer – you know, second-hand. Then we could go all over the Heath. I've told the others . . .'

'Great,' said Paul. 'We've got bikes but they're in the country. I think we'd be allowed them up here though, with the Heath.'

'OK. See you then,' said Michael, and he put his hands in his pockets and walked on down the hill, whistling. They watched him go and then turned into Brownlow Street.

By the gate of Number 25 Neville stopped. 'Glad it all turned out all right,' he said. Jo nodded and grinned, hugging Kipper close.

'Just think,' said Jo as they reached the gate of Number 35, 'this time last week we hadn't even found the cubs.'

Paul nodded. 'And now we've rescued them, and kept them a secret, and lost Kipper . . .'

'And found him again,' Jo interrupted.

'And become members of the gang.' They stared at one another.

'Wow!' said Jo. 'What a week!'

'I know,' said Paul. 'I feel as though everything's beginning all over again. London won't be so bad after all, will it Jo?'

'Not half bad,' said Jo, kissing Kipper's nose.

17

Wood End Grove

One sunny morning not long after that, Mr Tomlinson took the whole family to Wood End Grove to look at a house. It was opposite the dairy and was small, only four rooms, two up and two down, with a kitchen and bathroom built on at the back. The garden was tiny, too, but it was close to the Heath and it was empty.

Mrs Tomlinson stalked all over the house looking suspicious and opening cupboard doors and peering into corners. But she noticed the honeysuckle in the back garden and the view of the Heath from the back bedroom, and the bright airiness of the rooms, even though they were so small. At last she said, 'Bit small, but it has a good feel to it.' She sniffed. 'Better than that other place.'

Then she peered out of the open front door up and down the street which was flooded with sunshine. The baby in the next-door garden sat up in its pram and gurgled at her, bringing a smile to her eyes. Farther down the row an old man was putting crumbs out for the birds. 'Yes,' she said. 'I reckon it'll just about do, this will.'

Her husband smiled at her and then, looking at Paul and Jo he said, 'Of course, we don't have to stay in London. But if we do decide to, then this might . . .'

' 'Course we're going to stay,' Jo interrupted.

Mr Tomlinson raised his eyebrows. 'I thought you two hated London,' he said, with a twinkle in his eye.

'We did,' said Paul slowly. 'We don't any more, do we Jo?'

'No,' said Jo. 'It's OK.'

'That's right,' Paul nodded. 'London's OK.'

So it was settled and they took a lease on the house. Mr Tomlinson was delighted because it meant that he could stay on with the firm in London, where the prospects were good. Mrs Tomlinson was delighted and lost no time in introducing herself to all her neighbours who seemed quite a different sort of people from that unfriendly lot in Brownlow Street, she told her husband. And Paul and Jo were delighted because the Heath was so close that it was really their back garden, and they could wander out there whenever they wanted to, almost as though they were in the country again.

But when the move was over and the family were all installed, Cottontail and Kipper were more delighted than any of them; all the sights and sounds and scents of the Heath were there, at their doorstep. It became a customary sight for the residents of Wood End Grove to see Paul and Jo leading the two frisking cubs down the street towards the Heath, and disappearing through the iron posts at the end.

The cubs had become more fox-like in appearance now. Their legs were longer, their ears larger and more pricked, and their tails were filling out too, so that they looked more like the fully grown fox's brush. At first Paul and Jo always kept them on leads when they went on the Heath, fearful in case the cubs should run away, though they were very affectionate still. They had their own kennel which Mr Tomlinson had built in the back garden, for they smelt too strongly to be kept in the house. They often came in, however, and would sit with the family at meal times, greedy for whatever scraps might be passed down to them from the table.

As spring lengthened into summer the cubs became restless. Paul was bewildered by the change in their behaviour, but Jo understood only too well what was causing it. The cubs wanted to be out on the Heath, alone. They wanted to hunt and explore and run wild. They were growing up.

One day Jo came down early and found that Cottontail had escaped from the back garden. Always the larger and stronger of the two, he was now a half-grown dog fox and was big enough to jump up on the wall. From there it was easy enough to reach the Heath, since the back wall of the garden abutted on to an alleyway which led directly there.

Jo wasn't worried. He was sure that Cottontail would come back, and he was right. When the boys returned from school, they found both cubs in the back garden as usual, Cottontail looking very smug.

Jo looked at the wall and then he looked at Kipper. Kipper had turned out to be a vixen, and had, therefore, remained the smaller of the two cubs. But Jo could see that despite that Kipper would soon be able to get over the wall as well and the time had come when they must make a decision. Either they could let the cubs come and go at will, hoping that they would return after their expeditions, or they could build a higher fence and try to keep them in, like animals in a zoo.

Paul was spending more and more time with the gang nowadays, especially since the bicycles had arrived from Martinford. He still loved the cubs, of course, but not quite in the way that Jo did, and the cubs didn't need so much attention now that they were bigger. So Jo decided to think things over by himself before talking to Paul.

Several days later both cubs disappeared, and returned after a long foraging expedition. Jo knew that they had been hunting, because they refused their dinner that night. He had to talk to Paul.

'I think we shall have to cut down on the food we give them,' he said.

'Why should we do that?' Paul asked.

'They're learning to hunt now,' said Jo sadly. 'They go over the wall quite often. We can't keep them locked up can we?'

'Do you think they'll go off for good?'

'I don't suppose so. Not yet, anyway.'

'I think we should let them hunt,' said Paul, after thinking for a moment. 'I mean they are wild animals really, aren't they?'

So it was decided. Sometimes there were bones about in the garden after that, and once Mrs Tomlinson found a half-eaten pigeon in the flower bed which made her scream.

Jo tried not to think too much about where the cubs went. He worried about the railway line though, and the cars on the roads. He hoped that they always stayed well out on the Heath, away from danger. Often he walked alone on the Heath himself hoping to see them and watch what they did. During one of these walks he found a thrush with a broken wing which he brought home and nursed back to health. It helped to take his mind off the cubs.

With the approach of the summer holidays, the boys had to talk the whole thing over with their parents. They were going to Martinford for two weeks and they couldn't possibly take Cottontail and Kipper with them.

Jo was worried about leaving them for so long without food, although now they seldom ate what was put down for them and only came to the kennel to sleep. Mrs Tomlinson said that she was sure they would be all right while the family were away and everyone agreed, except Jo.

'The house will be empty and shut up,' he said gloomily. 'They'll think we've deserted them.'

In the end Jo slipped next door and asked their neighbour, Mrs Norrington, if she would put food down for the cubs. Mrs Norrington was a widow and lived alone. She had always been interested in the cubs and when Jo asked her she was delighted to help and listened carefully while he explained what had to be done.

'Though I don't suppose they'll eat much food,' Jo said wistfully. 'They do almost all their own hunting now, you see. Like real wild foxes in the country,' he added. He was proud of Cottontail and Kipper, although not having them around so much made him sad as well.

'Well, you have a good holiday with your Granny and don't worry,' said Mrs Norrington kindly. 'I'll see that the cubs get their food.' She had no grandchildren of her own, and she had taken a fancy to Jo, partly because of his fondness for animals, which she shared. She had five cats.

When they came back Mrs Norrington said that the food had gone once or twice, but she hadn't seen the cubs at all. She also said that Jo could have one of her kittens which had been born to her tortoiseshell cat while they were away.

Soon it was autumn. Once or twice, coming down early, the boys would find a cub asleep in the kennel, but as the nights became longer their visits were more

155

and more infrequent. Once, walking on the Heath alone, Jo met Kipper. The cub came up to him, laid her nose in the palm of his hand briefly and then trotted off, looking once over her shoulder towards Jo.

One perfect autumn evening, when all the trees had turned golden and toffee-coloured, and the sky was clear and changing from palest blue to misty grey, Mr Tomlinson and Paul and Jo walked over towards the far side of the Heath. Breasting the rise of a hill before the others Jo was in time to see a fox galloping along beside a thick plantation of rhododendrons; the fox's coat was full, its tail thick and heavy and it moved with long-legged graceful ease, russet-coloured against the dark green of the shrubs.

'Look,' Jo called. 'Kipper.'

The others were in time to see the vixen lift her head for a moment, listening to the sound of Jo's voice, and then turn and disappear among the bushes.

'Gone,' Jo whispered. 'Gone.'

Mr Tomlinson laid his hand on his son's shoulder. 'Never mind, Jo,' he said. 'I reckon you made a good job of those foxes – both of you. I daresay that letting them go was harder than catching them, wasn't it?'

'Yes,' said Jo thoughtfully. 'It was. We could have built up a wall in the garden I suppose. But it wouldn't have been right, would it?'

'Like a zoo,' said Paul.

'No doubt about it,' said Mr Tomlinson, 'you've done the right thing.'

'Cheer up, Jo,' said Paul. 'Something else will turn up. Something always does.'

'Better be making for home,' said Mr Tomlinson. 'Your mother will be wondering where we are.'

The bright lights of the city were spread out before

them as they turned back, and they were part of it now. They were Londoners.

So then it really was over. Except that sometimes on frosty nights when Paul and Jo were neither asleep nor awake, but between the two, they would hear the clear, sharp bark of a fox out on the Heath, and an answering bark from farther away, and slipping back into sleep again they knew that the foxes, their foxes, were still out there, hunting and calling and running free under the velvet twinkling sky.

Penelope Lively

Astercote 25p

Two children enter a forbidden wood haunted by memories of a
village wiped out by the Black Death. When sickness comes to
their village its inhabitants seem to remember the time of the
plague and let superstition take over. A powerful, evocative
fantasy.

The Whispering Knights 25p

Susie, Martha and William concoct a witch's brew over a fire in
an old barn. They do not expect anything to happen but what
they do not know is that the barn is an old haunt of witches and
should be treated with respect!

Publishing soon:

The Wild Hunt of Hagworthy

The dancers rehearse, with medieval costumes and antlered
masks; in Hagworthy in Somerset the ancient Horn Dance has
been revived to raise money for the church fete. Then rumours
start. The Wild Hunt has been heard again – ghost hounds and
antlered horsemen – brought back by the revival of the Horn
Dance.

Maria Gripe

Josephine 25p
Hugo 25p
Hugo and Josephine 25p

An endearing trilogy about two children, humorously and
sensitively told.

Lavinia Derwent

Sula 25p
Return to Sula 25p

Two charming tales about a boy's adventures on a remote
Scottish Island.

Anne de Roo

Cinnamon and Nutmeg 30p

Two young animals are rescued from the New Zealand bush by a
young girl on the scent of a mystery involving the close-knit
farming community on the borders of the Taranaki plain.

Piccolo non-fiction

Piccolo All The Year Round Book 50p
Deborah Manley

Collecting Things 30p
Elizabeth Gundrey

Amazing Scientific Facts 25p
Jane Sherman

Blue Peter Special Assignment: Venice and Brussels 25p
Dorothy Smith and Edward Barnes

Blue Peter Special Assignment: Madrid, Dublin and York 25p
Dorothy Smith and Edward Barnes

Piccolo Encyclopedia of Sport 40p
Peter Mathews

Piccolo Encyclopedia of Useful Facts 40p
Jean Stroud

These and other Piccolo books are obtainable from all booksellers
and newsagents. If you have any difficulty please send
purchase price plus 10p postage to

PO Box 11 Falmouth Cornwall

While every effort is made to keep prices low, it is sometimes
necessary to increase prices at short notice. Pan Books reserve
the right to show new retail prices on covers which may differ
from those previously advertised in the text or elsewhere.